DOUBLE PLAY
AT SHORT

The #1
Sports Series
for Kids

Matt Christopher

DOUBLE PLAY
AT SHORT

Little, Brown and Company
Boston   New York   London

First Paperback Edition

The characters and events portrayed in this book are fictitious. Any similarity to real persons, living or dead, is coincidental and not intended by the author.

Matt Christopher™ is a trademark of Catherine M. Christopher.

Library of Congress Cataloging-in-Publication Data

Christopher, Matt.
    Double play at short / by Matt Christopher. — 1st ed.
        p.   cm.
    Summary: Twelve-year-old Danny thinks that there is something very familiar about the girl who plays shortstop on the team he faces during the championship series, and his curiosity leads him to a surprising discovery about his own adoption.
    ISBN 0-316-14201-8
    [1. Baseball — Fiction.   2. Adoption — Fiction.
3. Twins — Fiction.]   I. Title.
PZ7.C458Dpn   1995
[Fic] — dc20   94-39170

10 9 8 7

COM-MO

Printed in the United States of America

To
Bruce
and
Ann

Thwap!

The ball settled solidly in the cup of Danny Walker's well-oiled glove.

"Lucky!" called out Joel Jackson, his best buddy and the Bullets' center fielder.

"Nah, just talented," said Danny with a big smile. He pegged the ball over to Frankie Snow, the Bullets' relief infielder, then gazed around the field. All his teammates were keyed up, but he was relaxed.

He could afford to be. Danny Walker was a natural — on the field as well as at bat.

As the Bullets continued their warm-up, he felt great. Today was the first game in their five-game championship series against the Jaguars. That alone made the warm-up more intense than usual. Add to that the fact that the players' stats for this series

1

would help determine who'd be chosen for the county All-Star team, and you got a pressure-filled situation.

Baseballs whizzed from player to player in every direction. A few got dropped. Sometimes a player even got bopped accidentally by a teammate.

But Danny was always on the alert. His muscles were poised and ready to respond to any ball that came in his direction.

"Way to go, Danny," called his friend Joanne Bell, the Bullets' first baseman, as he scooped up another one of Joel's throws.

Danny spun around and hurled the ball in her direction. Joanne stretched forward and snagged the ball in the elongated cup of her trapper's mitt. She was really sharp at first base.

But not as consistent as Danny was at shortstop. He seemed made for the position. He stood about five feet, four inches high, and he was solid, without an ounce of fat. With his strong arms and legs, he could get low to the ground or leap high into the air. Whatever it took to get the ball or stop the runner between second and third, Danny was right there.

He even wore his wavy, dark auburn hair cut short so it wouldn't flop in his eyes and get in his way.

Danny was the Bullets' top hitter. He had more hits and runs batted in than any other player on the team. And he was just as valuable on the field. The combination of hitting and fielding made him an almost sure pick for the county All-Star team.

The umpire's whistle blew. It was time for the game to begin. Danny tossed one more ball over to the Bullets' third baseman, Mike Worsley, then headed toward the dugout. He lined up with the rest of the Bullets as the scratchy sound of "The Star-Spangled Banner" poured out of the loudspeakers.

"Play ball!" the ump shouted when the music stopped.

The Bullets were first at bat. Vern Labar, their second baseman, jogged over to the plate. Danny moved to the far side of the dugout. He leaned on one knee and watched Vern crouch down into his batting position.

The first pitch was high. Vern wisely let it go by.

The next one was down the middle. Vern swung at it and missed.

Then, with the count at 1 and 1, the pitcher released one that was a little bit inside, just the way Vern liked them. He swung at it and connected. The ball went sizzling by the pitcher's mound and took a high bounce. It looked as though it would squeeze through the hole just to the left of second base.

But the Jaguars' shortstop was too fast. A streak of white with green edges, she snagged the ball in her outstretched glove and pulled it in. Danny could see her auburn ponytail flying behind her cap as she quickly pegged the ball to first base for the out.

Boy, she's fast on her feet, he thought. He made a mental note to keep the ball away from the general vicinity of shortstop.

Unlike some kids, who studied every statistic about every game and memorized scores and standings, Danny's great interest in baseball had always been right on the diamond. He knew who was who in the league and where the Bullets stood in terms of games ahead or behind, but he didn't spend a whole lot of time analyzing those things. He sized up the opposing team right off during a game, then let his intuition take over. After all, relying on his instincts made him a sharp infielder. That, and his strong batting average, made him a real asset to any team — including the All-Stars, he hoped.

Elaine Norbert, the Bullets' right fielder, was up next. She was tall and skinny, and the Bullets' uniform, white and blue trim, made her seem even taller. She looked as though the gentlest little breeze could knock her over. But somehow or other, Elaine sure had a way of scaring pitchers. Instead of taking advantage of the big strike zone, they ended up handing her the ball on a silver platter.

Danny flopped down on the bench to watch the action from a different area of the dugout. As usual, he just couldn't sit still now that the game had started. "Antsy," his dad called him. "You've got ants in your pants, Danny," he'd say.

The first pitch to Elaine was so low, it almost raised up the dust in front of the plate. Danny smiled to himself as he saw Elaine scowl at Andy Hooten, the Jaguars' pitcher.

"Looks like Elaine's starting to work him over right away," said Joel Jackson, seated next to Danny on the bench. "I don't know how she does it."

"She just acts tough. And they fall for it," said Danny.

5

"Hey, whatever works," said Joel.

It didn't surprise either boy that the second pitch was right where Elaine wanted it — straight down the middle.

Her bat connected solidly, and the ball took off over the second baseman's head and into the grass. The right fielder came running in and stopped it from going farther. He threw to first, but Elaine was already on base, tucking her hair under her blue cap.

Good, thought Danny. That means we have a chance of scoring a run right off in the first inning. And there's a chance I'll get to bat, too. I hope I can add another hit to my stats. Every little bit helps!

Next up for the Bullets was Mike Worsley, the team's third baseman.

"Come on, Mike," Danny shouted. "Drive her home!"

He said the words, but deep down he didn't really think much of Elaine's chance of crossing the plate. Mike was a terrific fielder, but his hitting had fallen off lately and he was clearly in a slump. Mike had struck out three times in the last pre-series game the Bullets had played just last week.

This time, he surprised everyone. He connected solidly on the third pitch. For a moment it looked as though the ball would go over the fence for a home run. Then, suddenly, it dropped — right into the mitt of the Jaguars' left fielder, Wally Mills. Wally pegged it to second, but he was too late. Elaine slid safely under the second baseman's glove.

Danny noticed that the Jaguars' shortstop had covered the play just right. She was in a position, all set to make the tag, in case Elaine tried to go farther.

In fact, he found that he was watching the shortstop position almost more than the action at the plate. Ken Hunter, the Bullets' left fielder, took his turn at bat. Ken was a little short for a twelve-year-old and crouched in at the plate real tight. That didn't give pitchers much of strike zone to go for. It usually made for some tricky calls by the ump, too.

The first pitch was much too high. Ball one.

The next pitch surprised everyone. A meatball right down the middle, it went for a called strike. Ken stepped back from the plate, rubbed his hands on his chunky thighs, then moved back into position.

Crouched on one knee in the on-deck circle,

Danny sent his teammate a silent signal. Pay attention, buddy. Eyes sharp.

It seemed like Ken picked up on his message. He swung at the next pitch and hit a long, long, long, high fly ball — that fell just outside the third base line. Foul!

The Jaguars' third baseman chased after the ball, which had landed midway between him and left field. For a moment, it had looked as though Elaine might try to advance to third. But the Jaguars' shortstop had put an end to any such idea. She was right there, covering the position, glove extended for any throw that might come her way.

With a 1 and 2 count, the Jaguars had a shot at retiring the Bullets right then and there. But they missed their chance. As Ken hunkered down at the plate, the next three pitches were all over the place. The ump called them, and Ken got a walk. He dropped his bat and trotted down the line to first base.

Two runners on base. As Danny came up to bat, he knew that he had a good chance to put the Bullets on the scoreboard. That would give the team a great psychological advantage for the whole series.

"Come on, Danny!" he heard a voice cheer from the stands. He recognized the sound of his older sister, Jennifer. Although she was all wrapped up with her work as the editor of the school newspaper, she still tried to make as many of his games as possible.

Both Danny and Jennifer had been adopted when they were infants. But they were as close as any biological brother and sister. In fact, Mrs. Walker used to joke with them and say, "If I knew that you kids would turn out so well, we would have put in for a dozen just like you."

But Danny wasn't thinking about that now. He scuffled his toe in the dirt next to the plate, hefted the bat into position over his left shoulder, and gazed out into the field. He knew some pitchers had trouble throwing to lefties — and since Danny fielded righty, they usually weren't prepared for him to take a left-handed stance.

But today was different. The pitcher didn't even hesitate.

"Strike!"

Danny scowled and stepped out of the batter's box. He eyed the pitcher but shifted his gaze slightly to the left when a blaze of red hair caught his attention. Even though Danny wasn't in the box, the Jaguars' shortstop was hunkered down in position. She shifted from one foot to the other, her ponytail swinging out behind her. She looked ready for anything.

For some reason, she made Danny uneasy.

"Play ball!"

Danny started at the umpire's call. It wasn't like him to let his mind wander during a game.

Hey, take your own advice, Walker, he said to himself. Pay attention! He moved back to the plate and gripped the bat. He was ready.

The ball was coming straight toward him. He had just enough time to respond to what looked like his kind of pitch. Instinct took over.

Danny swung hard.

At first, it felt like a solid hit coming off his bat. But there wasn't that zing of tension, that snapping crack that signaled the long ball he wanted to send over the fence. Instead, this hit was much too high and much too close to home plate. It was an easy pick for Drew Ferris, the Jaguars' catcher, who bagged it for the Bullets' third and final out.

2

Danny shook his head as he grabbed his mitt and headed out for the diamond.

"You'll get 'im next time," said Elaine. She gave him a playful poke and ran off toward right field.

"Thanks, slugger," Danny said. He was disappointed that he hadn't done so well his first time up. He would have liked the little edge that came with getting on the scoreboard first.

But right now he had to do his best to keep the Jaguars from scoring. Glancing to either side to make sure Mike was set at third base and Vern at second, he readied himself for the first pitch.

Joey Sands was up. Danny could tell from his tense stance Joey was ready to belt the ball. In fact, Joey was too tense — he swung at a ball that almost dusted the plate. That must have settled him down a little, because he let the next three pitches, all balls, go by. Still, Danny was ready to make a move on any ball that came his way.

With a 3 and 1 count, Joey could afford to wait the next one out. But he couldn't resist a breaking ball that seemed to have his name on it. He swung and connected.

If it had dropped a little sooner or later, it probably would have been a hit. As it happened, it was a hard drive to short. With an easy motion, Danny caught the ball fair and square for the first out.

As the Jaguars shuffled around in the dugout, Danny glimpsed shiny auburn hair slipping here and there. She sure doesn't stay put in the dugout, he thought. I know how she feels.

Wally Mills, the Jaguars' left fielder, was a power hitter. The entire infield backed up when he came to bat next. But Marc Bailey, the Bullets' pitcher, got two called strikes by him before Wally connected with the ball. It was a rocket down the first base line, but Joanne was on top of it like a cat on a mouse. She tagged the base before Wally could drop his bat.

Following her usual routine after a quick out, Joanne pegged the ball across to Danny. But Danny was watching the Jaguars' dugout. The ball went right by him, and Joel had to run in to grab it and pass it on to Larry Chuan behind the plate.

"Heads up, Walker!" called Joel. That got Danny's attention. He shifted his eyes back toward the plate, where Marsha Kerns was settling in to her batting stance.

The second baseman for the Jaguars was a specialist in placing the ball wherever she found a weakness. So far, the Bullets hadn't given her much to aim for, but they weren't taking any chances. All eyes were on Marsha.

Marc threw two pitches that were way outside. Then, with a 2 and 0 count, he delivered a meatball, and she found it.

Crack!

The Bullets' outfield ran backward, but it was no use. The ball was over the fence. The fans cheered as the score went up: Jaguars 1, Bullets 0.

Danny was sorry to see the Jaguars score first.

But it's just the start of the game, he thought. And the series, too, he added.

Marsha's homer shook Marc's confidence a little. He got the next batter, Roy Feenie, to swing at one inside pitch, but the next four throws were clearly balls. Ray dropped his bat and jogged down to first base as the Jaguars' shortstop stepped up to the plate. Her long red ponytail swayed back and forth until she tucked it away and settled the bat a few inches above her shoulder.

Hey, Danny noticed with surprise, she bats lefty. I could have sworn I saw her throwing with her right hand. Boy, I wonder if she's copying me!

Facing his left-handed hitter, Marc was a little cautious. After throwing three balls in a row, he baited her into swinging at an outside pitch she should have passed up. But she leaned into her swing and managed to hit the ball just over Joanne and into the grass behind first base. Roy took off toward second. Danny came in to cover him if he tried for third, but he held up as the batter arrived safely on first.

Who is she? Danny wondered. I thought I knew most of the players in the league, but I don't re-member ever seeing her before. Must be new.

His curiosity was interrupted by the action at the plate. Marc had settled down a little and was sizzling them by Al Norris, the Jaguars' center fielder. After

14

two strikes, he went for the third pitch and clobbered the ball. It flew high, but not far. And when it
landed, it was smack in the middle of Vern Labar's
glove for the third out.

On his way off the field, Danny took a good look
at the Jaguars' shortstop. She was thumping her
fist into her glove, waiting to catch a few warm-up
throws. He saw that he had remembered correctly —
she *did* field right-handed, although she batted lefty.
Just like he did.

"Hey, Walker!" Joel's call interrupted Danny's
thoughts. "I thought you were the only ambidextrous shortstop in the league. Looks like you and
that girl have a lot in common."

As Danny watched her shag a few balls, he had a
disturbing thought. What if this girl was like him in
other ways, too? What if she was just as good a
baseball player as he was? He knew her abilities
would make the series championship more of a
challenge — but would that make her a threat to his
chances for the All-Star squad?

He took a seat next to Joel and said, "Yeah, we
redheads are all alike. I guess that means I'll be
knocking a nice high line drive over first."

"Couldn't hurt," said Joel.

They settled down on the bench to see what the lower half of the Bullets' batting order could do to put them back in the game.

Joanne did the team proud by belting the ball for a stand-up triple. Her long legs were too fast for the throw from deep right field. Then Joel hit a foul ball that the Jaguars' third baseman caught in the air for the first out.

Larry sneaked a hit by the Jaguars' pitcher and sped to first for a single, but it wasn't enough to bring Joanne home. So Marc came to bat with runners at first and third.

None of the Bullets expected a lot from their pitcher's hitting. With one away, they just wanted him to get it over with so the top of the order could get a shot.

But their worst fears came true. Marc hit a double play, and the inning ended with two players having reached base but no score for the Bullets.

Danny watched the red-haired shortstop run in. Curiosity overwhelmed him. He decided he had to find out who she was. He grabbed his glove, and as he headed out toward the field, he stopped by the end of the bench where Frankie Snow, the infield sub, had the scorecard. Glancing down the lineup, he saw that her name was Tammy Aiken.

Huh! Never heard of her, he thought. Never heard of anybody called Aiken. She must be new to the league.

He ran off to take up his position, determined to put her out of his mind.

In the second inning, Marc's pitching was off the mark a lot. He walked two batters and gave up one hit before retiring the side. It was enough to give the Jaguars their second run on the scoreboard.

When the Bullets came up to bat in the third inning, Vern popped a short one to right field for the first out. Elaine got on base with a walk, but then Mike hit a long ball to center field that was caught for the second out. Ken Hunter came up to bat and yielded the first strikeout for Andy Hooten, ending the Bullets' chances that inning.

At first, it looked to Danny like Marc was getting his stuff back. He put away Roy Feenie one-two-three to show he could strike out a batter, too. But then that shortstop for the Jaguars, the one called Aiken, came up to bat. Danny's eyes were glued to her. He took in her every move.

She tucked her ponytail under and wiped her hands together before she picked up the bat. Then she scuffled her forward toe into position, putting most of her weight on her back leg. She crouched in wait for the pitch.

Something about the way she stood bothered him, but he couldn't figure out what it was.

After letting two bad pitches go by, Tammy swung at the next one. She missed it, but he could see the power behind her swing. It paid off with the next pitch. She connected for a hit deep into right field that she pushed into a double.

Al Norris, the Jaguars' center fielder, didn't give her a chance to move any farther. He popped out to third base, and the Bullets held the runner in check.

They weren't so lucky with the next batter. Drew Ferris got a single off Marc, and the Aiken girl made it easily to third.

With two outs and runners on first and third, the Bullets had their work cut out for them. Danny hoped they would hold off another run scoring.

He was disappointed. Millie Albright, the Jaguars' right fielder, hit the ball into short right for a single. The runner on third scored, and the runner on first advanced to third. It was now 3 to 0 on the scoreboard.

Luckily, Andy Hooten was no better at bat than Marc Bailey. The Jaguars' pitcher went down swinging for the third out.

Danny was the leadoff hitter for the Bullets in the fourth inning. He was determined to get a hit — to get the ball rolling, so to speak.

He did — in a big way. On the first pitch, a fastball right down the middle, he clobbered the ball. The ball climbed high and curved slightly as it soared over the left field fence. A home run! At long last, the Bullets were on the scoreboard.

As Danny rounded the bases, he could hear his sister's voice loud and clear over the roar of the crowd. "That's my baby bro!" she yelled.

But that was the only run the Bullets earned that inning. Joanne followed Danny's homer with a single, but the next three batters went down in a row to close out the Bullets' chances of catching up that inning.

The Jaguars went scoreless for the first time in the fourth inning. Marc got his third strikeout on Wally Mills, but he gave up two hits. There were runners on first and second when Tammy Aiken came up to bat. She took it to a full count before she popped one high into the air down the third base line. Mike was waiting to make the catch. He then pegged the ball to second, where the runner was tagged off base for the third and final out.

The fifth inning did nothing to improve the Bullets' score. Vern led off. Four bad pitches later, he walked down the line to first base. But then Elaine grounded out, and he stayed where he was. Mike hit a long fly ball that was caught by the Jaguars' right fielder, but Vern got to second base safely. Then Ken connected for a single, and Vern advanced to third on the play.

It was Danny's turn at bat. He could practically taste a scoring hit. He dug his forward toe into the dirt and crouched down low, weight slightly back. As the pitch came his way, it looked like a good one. He swung.

Wuff!

"Strike!"

20

He almost toppled over from the power behind his swing. But he caught himself and adjusted his helmet as he got ready for the next pitch. It was way out of the striking range. So were the next three. Danny dropped his bat and headed down to first base.

The bases were now loaded. It was a perfect setup for a rally by the Bullets. The fans roared their encouragement. But unfortunately, Joanne popped one up to the Jaguars' pitcher, and the cheers from the stands and dugout died.

Disaster — that was the word Danny figured the Bullets could have used to describe the fifth inning while the Jaguars were at bat. Marc pitched two strikeouts, but he also walked two batters. A big three-bagger by Joey Sands did the job, scoring two more runs for the Jaguars to put them ahead 5 to 1, before the side was retired.

The Bullets couldn't pull this one out. In the sixth and final inning, Joel struck out. Larry and Marc each got on base, but Vern and Elaine finished the game off with two lackluster hits that were easily tagged out by the up and running Jaguars. The fans applauded the end of the game.

Leaving the dugout, Danny could see an auburn ponytail bobbing up and down as the winning team scrambled off the field. For some reason, the sight of Tammy Aiken celebrating with her teammates depressed him almost as much as the loss of the first championship game did. He knew her talents had helped win the game for the Jaguars.

Who is she? he thought angrily. And why did she have to show up now?

3

The Bullets didn't linger long in the locker room after the game. Everyone seemed like they were in a big rush to put this game behind them. Danny was usually one of the first to change into his street clothes and leave. Today he was one of the last. When he got outside, he saw his sister, Jennifer, leaning on the handlebars of her bicycle right next to the rack where all the players parked theirs. There was only one bike left: his.

"Come on," she said. "I'll ride home with you."

At fourteen, Jennifer was a little taller than Elaine. With her long, straight black hair, hazel eyes, and dark complexion, she didn't look much like Danny's sister. But since they'd grown up together since infancy, they acted exactly the way an older sister and a younger brother might be expected to: They fought like the dickens once in a while but cared a lot about each other. Most of the time they were as close as two peas in a pod, as their mother commented when they were off by themselves.

"Tough game," she said, turning her bike in the direction of the Walker home.

Jennifer was a real baseball freak and came to almost every one of his games. Sometimes she managed to drag one of her girlfriends along with her. She was on the field hockey team and kept herself in good condition by running and regular workouts. When Jennifer's team played during the fall season, Danny managed to get out for her games, too. It was the sort of thing they did for each other automatically.

Danny shook his head. "Yeah," he replied. "We just couldn't seem to get anything going."

"I could tell," Jennifer said. "Hey, but you got that homer. That ought to keep you in the running, you know, for the All-Stars." She braked suddenly and swung off her bike. "Wait a sec, I have to fix my toe guards. They keep slipping. Now the way I figure it . . ."

Jennifer launched into a long speech about the

odds on Danny making the county All-Star team. She was a whiz at math and had a habit of calculating all the team statistics. This wasn't the first time she had expounded her theory on why he was a sure bet.

But he was only half listening to her. She hopped back on her bike, and they pedaled along the road from the baseball field. His thoughts kept springing back to the Jaguars' shortstop.

Was he the only one who'd noticed her? Other than Joel, who was always making wisecracks, none of the other guys on the Bullets team had said anything to make him think they thought she was better than he was. In fact, they seemed a little distant today. Usually, even after a loss, there was a lot of joking back and forth in the locker room. But today they were all kind of silent and moving like they were in a big hurry.

Maybe it had to do with the series getting off to a rough start. He sure would have liked to have won today's game. Now they had to play catch-up to win the championship. And the Jaguars were not going to be pushovers. They had solid hitting and fielding — like that redheaded shortstop.

There she was again. He had to find out if Jennifer had noticed her. But if he came right out with it, she might think he was worried about the competition. And he wasn't — was he? No, he had to be real cool. Just like those guys in the whodunits on TV.

"So, Jen, you think I have a shot, huh? Great," he said. "Gee, it'd be tough to pick an All-Star team out of today's game, don'tcha think? I mean, nobody did all that great, right? Like, there wasn't anybody on the Jaguars who really, really stood out, right?"

"Actually, Danny, a funny thing happened," Jennifer said, signaling a left turn. They were about three blocks from home, and the roads narrowed a little as they approached their neighborhood.

"Funny?" he asked. "What do you mean 'funny'? I didn't think the game was a million laughs."

"Come on, Danny, don't get all twisted up over one lost game," Jennifer said. "Relax a little, huh? I was just going to say that during the third inning, I took my eyes off the game for a minute. When I looked up, I could have sworn I saw you crossing the plate. But it wasn't you. It was the Jaguars' shortstop. Come to think of it, a similar thing happened

26

when she came to bat — her stance was a lot like yours. But maybe that's the way *all* right-hand fielders/left-hand batters stand. Anyhow, it was funny the way I made that mistake. She's pretty good, but you're still the best."

"Joel gave me a zing about the same thing — her being ambidextrous like me, I mean. I told him it was the red hair that confused him."

"Good reply!" she said, laughing. "That Joel doesn't miss much. Hey, listen, don't let that shortstop get to you."

"Nah, don't worry," said Danny. "But I guess she's pretty good, huh?"

"She's okay," said Jennifer. "She only played the last few games with them. I mean, I didn't come across her at the start of the season when I ran down the rosters."

"Oh, so you *have* heard of her before, though," he said, trying to sound casual. "You knew her name?"

"Danny, I know everyone's name," Jennifer said. "By the way — oh, first, want some gum?" She dug into her sweatshirt pocket with one hand as they rode along.

"Both hands," Danny warned her, nodding toward

the handlebar. The Walker kids had been drilled in bicycle safety and wore helmets even when they were just tooling around the road in front of their own house. "I don't want any gum right now. What were you going to say?"

"Okay, but wait a minute. I just want to fish this out of my pocket," said Jennifer, pulling off to the side of the road and burrowing in her sweatshirt for the gum. She popped a piece into her mouth and began chewing before she started pedaling again. "I was just going to tell you that my friend Loretta's father is on some committee or something with your coach, Mr. Lattizori. And Mr. Lattizori told Mr. Hinman, Loretta's father, that you're the best young player he's seen in a long time."

"He did? He said that?"

"Uh-huh. And he even said that you're a shoo-in for the All-Stars unless some real hot dog comes along. Those were his exact words," she said. "That's according to Loretta, who got it from her father, who got them from Mr. Lattizori. Sounds promising, doesn't it?"

"Yeah," he replied. "Sounds great."

The two of them rode along in silence. Danny wasn't saying anything, but he couldn't help but wonder. Could the Jaguars' shortstop be the unexpected "hot dog"?

He glanced over at Jennifer. At the same moment, she looked at him. They did it all the time. It was like they were reading each other's minds. The two of them began to laugh.

As they approached the Walker house, Danny had made up his mind. He wasn't going to make a big deal out of it. In fact, he probably wouldn't say anything to anyone. But all by himself, he was going to find out more about this redheaded hot dog named Tammy Aiken. He'd start by looking up her record.

They put away their bikes in the garage and headed for the back door.

"Wait a minute," said Jennifer. "I think Mom said there was some heavy stuff to take in off the front porch. Come on, I'll give you a hand."

"Stuff, who do you mean, 'stuff'?" he asked.

"I don't know," she answered. "Just some stuff. You know Mom. Probably some blankets or something from a catalogue."

"Blankets? You said it was heavy," he said.

"Danny, give me a break. Just come on around front and see what she wants," Jennifer snapped.

"Boy, you can really be a pain, you know," he grumbled. "Where's the stuff? I don't see anything."

They were on the front porch.

"Well, we're here — we might as well go in this way," she said. "After you."

"Thanks a whole lot," he said sarcastically.

He stepped inside the house and into the dark hallway. In an instant, a light was turned on and a chorus of voices shouted all at once, "Surprise! Happy birthday!"

Danny was stunned. He'd been thinking so much about the series and the All-Star team and the new shortstop that he'd completely forgotten what was happening that week.

It was two days before his twelfth birthday.

4

The house was packed. The whole Silver Bullets team was there along with some of Danny's other friends and Jennifer's, too. They all came over and slapped him on the back and gave him a few good-natured pokes in the ribs. Joel even called him "the old bullet." Nobody laughed. Sometimes Joel's jokes were weird. Anyhow, Danny was more interested in trying to hear what Loretta Hinman was saying. He could see her off in a corner talking to his father. He wondered if she was telling him what Coach Latti-zori had said to her father about him.

He tried to edge his way over there, but just then his mother came over. She gave him a big hug and a kiss.

"It's a little early, but we thought a party might be a good way to start off the series," she explained.

"And we knew we could get your friends on the team over here after the game."

"No wonder Jennifer kept stopping on the way home," he said.

"Your sister's pretty cool," said Vern.

"I had to stall so the pizza man could get here before we did," she said.

"Pizza! Great! What kind?" Joel asked.

"Everything but anchovies," Mr. Walker answered, laughing. "You kids can just pick out what you don't like."

Jennifer helped Mrs. Walker dish out slices of pizza to everyone. Mr. Walker went around handing out soft drinks. When everyone had some pizza and a soda, Mrs. Walker said to Danny, "I hope you like what we got you for your birthday." She pointed at a pile of presents stacked on top of a table near the front door.

"Wait a minute, his birthday isn't really today, you know," Jennifer protested.

"Come on, you want to see what's in those boxes just as much as I do," Danny said.

He went over and, with a little help from his pals, brought the presents into the living room. With Joel on one side and Jennifer on the other, he started opening them, beginning with a shoebox-looking package.

"You know, you guys really didn't have to — oh, boy, a package of new white sweat socks. Thanks a lot, Elaine," he said. I wonder what that's supposed to mean, he said to himself.

He opened the next package. It was a square box this time, from Mike. Inside was another stack of white sweat socks.

"Thanks, Mike. You and Elaine must shop at the same store," he said, laughing.

The next package he grabbed was some kind of tube or can, with a card from Larry. He popped open the lid and out came more white sweat socks.

"Wait a minute, are you guys trying to tell me something?" he asked.

The whole team broke up laughing. Then Joanne explained.

"Jennifer said that your mom and dad didn't want us to feel we had to bring presents. So we all decided to get you something you can really use."

"We went down the list," said Marc, "and you had every piece of sports equipment we could think of.

So we figured out the one thing no one ever gives you — and this was it. Can't have too many pairs of sweat socks, can you?"

"This is one guy who won't," said Danny, laughing. "You guys are really nuts. Are you sure there just wasn't a sale at the mall?"

"Wait a minute," said Jennifer. "There's more to open. Here's mine." She thrust a big flat package tied with a huge blue ribbon into his hands.

First he opened the card he found under the ribbon.

"Ah, mush," he said, turning a little red as he tucked the card in his shirt pocket. But he leaned over and gave her a kiss on the cheek. Then he unwrapped the package.

It was a scrapbook with his name in gold letters on the cover.

"You can put all your press clippings in it," said Jennifer.

"He's gonna have a lot of 'em when he makes the All-Stars," said Joel.

"Hey, don't jinx it!" shouted Elaine. "Let's see what else you got, Danny."

"Here's our present, Danny," said Mr. Walker,

handing him another beautifully wrapped package with a blue bow.

Again, Danny read the card before opening the package. He didn't say anything, but he looked a little teary as he gave his folks hugs.

When the wrapping came off, Danny was speechless. Inside the box he found a brand-new 35-millimeter camera, complete with zoom lens and strobe attachment. Danny had an inexpensive little snapshot camera, but this was more than he ever dreamed he might own.

"Hope you like it, son," said Mr. Walker.

All Danny could do was nod in silent appreciation.

"I guess it's time," Mrs. Walker said quietly to Jennifer, who disappeared into the kitchen. "All right, everyone, let's clear up a little of this mess."

She pushed an empty carton into the center of the room. Everyone pitched in by dumping the wrapping into it.

Joel wadded up a ball of tissue paper and tossed it in Danny's direction.

"Careful," said Joanne. "We don't want anything that'll burn around."

Just as she said that, the kitchen door opened and Jennifer came out with a big chocolate cake with white lettering on it. There were twelve candles all aglow in the frosting.

She put the cake down on the table in front of Danny. The house shook from the sound of all those voices singing "Happy Birthday." Then he blew all the candles out in one breath.

As the cake was being dished out, Joel shouted, "Speech! We want to hear from Mr. Birthday himself."

"No way!" said Danny. "I'll do my talking on the diamond!"

That brought a whole new chorus of razzing.

"Danny's all fired up 'cause he hit a home run!" shouted Joel. "He's heading for the majors."

"He'll have to beat out that redhead on the Jaguars first," said Jennifer, giving her brother a wink. "Little Miss Tammy Aiken might have a thing or two to do with it before he signs a contract."

"Tammy who?" asked Mr. Walker. He glanced quickly at Mrs. Walker.

"Tammy Aiken," said Jennifer. "She's the new shortstop for the Jaguars. She gave Danny a run for his money at short today. A real hot dog, if you ask me."

"Who asked you?" snapped Mrs. Walker suddenly. Jennifer stared at her open-mouthed. "Leave Danny alone about baseball," Mrs. Walker continued. "This is a birthday party. Everyone, have some more cake. Oh, I almost forgot the ice cream. I'll get it."

"Here, let me help you, Mrs. Walker," said Joanne.

"Thanks, but I can do it myself," said Mrs. Walker, rushing out of the room. Mr. Walker followed her silently into the kitchen.

Jennifer and Danny stared at each other. They shrugged their shoulders as if to say, What got into Mom?

5

There was no game the next day. Danny slept a little later than usual, and no one woke him.

When he did come into the kitchen for breakfast, he found a note propped up next to a bowl of cornflakes. "Gone out to do some shopping. Help yourself to breakfast. Lunch is in the fridge, too, if I'm not back. Hope you had a nice time at the party. Love, Mom."

Jennifer's bike helmet wasn't on the peg next to the door. She must have gone out already, too, Danny figured. And Dad's long at work by now. That's why it's so quiet around here, he realized as he munched away on his breakfast. Here it was his last day as an eleven-year-old, and he was all by himself. Well, what better time to do a little research into a certain shortstop?

He picked up the phone and dialed Joel's number.

"Hey, Joel, what's happening? Feel like taking a trip to the library? . . . Yeah, the library. I finished my summer reading, and I want to return some books and maybe look at some other stuff. Swing by and we'll ride over on our bikes."

By the time Danny had cleared up his breakfast things and collected his library books, Joel was at the back door honking on his bike horn. Joel loved old-fashioned gadgets. He was proud of the old rubber bulb squeeze horn he had mounted on his handle-bars.

"Come on, let's get the lead out," he called from outside.

Danny took his helmet off the peg and went out the back door.

"What's the big hurry?" he asked. "You afraid they're going to run out of *Dick and Jane*?"

"Wise guy," said Joel, smiling. He pointed at a stack of books in his bicycle basket. "I just want to get these back before I have to pay any more over-due fines on them."

The two boys set out for the ten-minute ride over to the county library. It was a large, modern limestone and glass building not far from the school and near the town line. Built with funds from the five towns that were part of the county, its central location made it a popular community cultural center for the area.

There was a bicycle rack near the side entrance. Danny and Joel got off their bikes and were wedging them into the rack when another kid rode up. It was Drew Ferris, the catcher for the Jaguars.

"Hey, suckers, how're you doin'?" he asked, slipping his bike into one of the slots in the rack. He took off his helmet and buckled it around the handlebars.

"Aren't you afraid someone will take that?" asked Danny, pointing at the helmet.

"Yeah, there must be some kids who need a helmet that expands for a swollen head," Joel added.

"A couple of comics," said Drew. "Listen are you guys here to look up the word *baseball* in the dictionary? 'Cause if you are, don't bother looking up the word *losers,* too. You'll find out what that means at the end of the series."

"One game isn't the series," said Joel defiantly.

"Like the old saying goes, it isn't over till the fat lady sings."

"She's going to be singing the blues for the Bullets," Drew said. "And when it's over, you're going to see a whole lot of county All-Stars coming from the Jaguars."

"Like, who, for instance?" asked Joel.

"Our new secret weapon, that's who," said Drew. "You haven't seen a thing yet. Wait till Tammy really hits her stride. She's going to eat up the shortstop spot on the All-Stars."

"Oh, yeah?" said Joel. "Well, ol' Danny here just might have something to say about that."

Danny felt the heat starting to rise from his shoulders up. He knew if he stood there, he'd turn beet red.

"I'll do my talking on the field," he said. "Come on, Joel, these books are growing moss on them."

He snatched the pile of books from his bike basket and headed into the dark hallway that led to the circulation desk.

He put his books on the returns counter and called to Joel, who had trailed after him. "I'm going

41

to look up some stuff in the newspaper room. I'll meet up with you in a little while."

"Okay, I want to see if they have the new *Baseball Illustrated* in the magazine rack. I'll find you when I'm through looking at it," said Joel.

Inside the newspaper room, Danny found a vacant microfilm machine that he could use to scan back issues of the *Jamestown Journal*. That was the hometown paper that carried news of the Jamestown Jaguars.

He started four months back, at the start of the baseball season. At that time, there was no mention of a shortstop named Tammy Aiken. That spot on the Jaguars' roster was filled by Marsha Kerns, their second baseman now.

He read all the stories about the Jaguars he could find. Then, just about four weeks ago, Tammy was first mentioned. She came in as a pinch hitter and drove home a winning run her first time at bat. From then on, it seemed that every story about the Jaguars mentioned her name.

Making the catch that won the game in the final inning was the Jaguars' new shortstop, Tammy Aiken.

A real tiger in the shortstop position, Aiken never seems to miss a ball hit in her direction.

The Jaguars are sizzling, and a lot of credit goes to their red-hot shortstop, Tammy Aiken.

The Jaguars are heading for the championship series with the Bullets, led by their number-one slugger, Tammy Aiken. The superstar shortstop who was adopted by her parents has now been adopted by Jamestown.

Adopted! Danny's eyes widened in surprise. Tammy Aiken was adopted, just like me!

"Hey Danny, what the heck are you looking at?" Joel's voice interrupted his thoughts.

Danny quickly clicked off the microfilm machine. For some reason, he didn't want Joel to see exactly what he was reading. "Um, it's just some old copies of the *Jamestown Journal* sports section. I — I wanted to check up a few of their past games and players."

Danny unloaded the reel of microfilm and put it away in its proper file. That's when he noticed Drew Ferris walking toward him.

"See you on the field, losers!" he hissed as Danny and Joel passed him.

43

"Not if we see you first," Joel retorted. Danny said nothing, but when he looked over his shoulder, he saw Drew walk into the newspaper room and open the file drawer Danny had closed moments ago.

As Danny and Joel walked near the checkout desk, Danny spotted a book on photography. He ducked into the aisle, pulled it off the shelf, and started flipping through it.

He was scanning the chapter titles when a familiar voice made him look up.

"Could you help me find some information on a local baseball team?" the voice asked.

Danny poked his head around the corner — and came face-to-face with his mother.

"Mom!" he cried. "What are you doing here?"

Mrs. Walker looked flustered. She opened her mouth to reply, but the librarian spoke before she had a chance to say anything.

"What is the name of the team you're interested in, ma'am?" she asked.

"What? Oh, never mind," Mrs. Walker said hurriedly. "Come on, Danny, Joel. Are your bikes out front? I'll walk you to them."

She took Danny's arm and led him away from the

desk. A few minutes later, she climbed into her car and waved good-bye. The boys unlocked their bikes, but before they started off, Joel spoke.

"What's with your mom?" he asked.

"I don't know," Danny replied truthfully. "She's been acting kind of strange lately, ever since my birthday party."

"Maybe she doesn't want you to grow up!" Joel said.

"Guess that's something *your* mom will never have to worry about!" Danny replied. He ducked to avoid Joel's playful swipe.

"Want to get a burger or something?" Joel asked.

"I don't think so," said Danny. "My mom left lunch for me in the fridge. I'd better have that. Then I think I'll do some work in her vegetable garden. You know, give her a little surprise."

"Are you okay, Danny? You hate working in the garden," said Joel.

Danny smiled at him. "I guess I'm just growing old," he said.

The two boys laughed and started pedaling down the road.

❖ ❖ ❖

Later that day, when Mrs. Walker arrived home, she was amazed to find her vegetable garden one hundred percent weed free.

"I don't know what got into you, Danny," she said. "But whatever it was, I'm glad of it. This lovely salad is all because of you." She passed a bowl of crisp greens and slices of deep red tomatoes around the dinner table that night.

"First a great baseball player, now a great gardener," Jennifer groaned. "I don't know how we live in the same house as you, Danny."

"Now if we can just get him to clean his room more often," Mr. Walker said.

"Ah, the tragic flaw," Jennifer announced. "So what else did you do all day while I was earning money baby-sitting, slugger?"

Danny told them that he and Joel had gone to the library to return some books.

"Joel isn't that hot on reading," he went on. "But he looked at some magazines while I looked at some old newspapers. By the way, Mom, what were *you* doing in the library today?"

"Speaking of books," Mrs. Walker said, ignoring his question. She reminded Mr. Walker about some shelves he was building for her in their living room. They started discussing whether they should be painted or stained.

"Checking out the competition?" Jennifer asked Danny while munching on a lettuce leaf.

"How'd you guess?" said Danny. "I read up on the Jaguars' shortstop. You're right, she's only been on the team for the last part of the season."

"Anything else?" Jennifer asked. "The paper have much to say about her?"

"The usual," he replied. "You know, 'Aiken is a superstar hitter and fielder' and all that. They also mentioned that Tammy was adopted."

Mr. and Mrs. Walker stopped talking. They looked at each other strangely. Then, for the second night in a row, Mrs. Walker rushed out of the room.

Jennifer broke the silence that followed. "What the heck is going on around here?"

6

The next day, the Bullets and the Jaguars met for the second game of the series. It was a bright, sunny, dry day without a cloud in the sky.

"Perfect baseball weather," Jennifer announced as she and Danny left for the field. "And I see you have your new camera. You ought to get some good pictures on a day like this. But how are you going to do that while you're playing?"

"I'm only going to use it during the warm-up."

He was true to his word. When the Bullets came out of the locker room for the start of the game, his camera hung by its strap around his neck.

"Hey, Danny, over here," said Joel. He crossed his eyes and stuck out his tongue.

Danny took his picture that way.

"Oh, Danny," called Elaine. She and Joanne stood arm in arm, leaning on their bats.

Danny took their picture.

Within a few minutes he had taken pictures of most of the team hanging around near the dugout. But eventually, they started tossing balls to each other. The warm-up was beginning. It was time to put away the camera.

But just before he took the strap from his neck, he held it up and gazed across the field through the lens. With his other hand he adjusted the zoom lens back and forth. It was amazing how close up it could make faraway things.

He swept across the diamond until a blur of auburn hair whizzed by his lens. He backed up, then zoomed in and saw Tammy waiting for a ball to come her way. He brought her face into focus and snapped the shutter.

Then he put the camera away. It was time to play.

The Jaguars led off. The Bullets had Ike Isaacs, a southpaw, on the mound. He'd be pitted against Eric Swan, a Jaguars left-handed pitcher.

Ike was a little tense starting off. He walked the

first batter but recovered his stuff and got ahead of the next with an 0 and 2 count. Jaguar left fielder Wally Mills went for the next pitch and popped an easy out to Vern at second.

But then Ike's real troubles began. He couldn't find the weakness in the next two batters. Each of them connected for a solid hit, first a triple, then a double. It was enough to drive in two runs.

With a runner on second, Tammy Aiken came up to bat. Danny stared across the field at her. All at once, he was struck by how similar her batting stance was to his. He used to study himself in the mirror, poised in that same position.

But there was something else about this girl that was bothering him. Even though he'd only seen her play in one game, everything about her suddenly seemed, well, *familiar.* But why?

Must be because I read so much about her yesterday, Danny reasoned. Then he shook his head. But now is not the time to be letting my mind wander! If the Jaguars get too far ahead this inning, it could spell real trouble for us. And if she gets a hit, her chances for the All-Star team get that much better, he added to himself.

Tammy let the first pitch, an inside breaker, go by for a called strike. Danny could see how intense she was by the way she stared straight down the line at Ike on the mound.

The next pitch was another inside breaker, but wider. Tammy went for it. The ball flew out toward left field well above Danny's head and too far in for Ken Hunter to catch in the air. Ken got it on a high bounce and went for the play at home.

But he was too late. The runner had scored and Tammy was safe on first. The score now read 3–0 for the Jaguars.

Even though it was early in the game, Coach Lattizori took a walk out to the mound to talk to Ike. Larry Chuan, the Bullets' catcher, tagged along. While they were conferring, Danny looked over to first. He was startled to see Tammy staring straight at him. She scowled and looked away before he had a chance to react.

I wonder what *that* was for, Danny thought.

When play resumed, Ike seemed to have recovered his confidence. He pitched two called strikes in a row to the next batter, Al Norris. Hungry for a hit, Al slashed at an outside pitch. He

51

barely tapped the ball for a pop-up foul caught by Larry.

But Tammy took advantage of the action around home plate to steal her way to second. When the Jaguars' catcher, Drew Ferris, came up to bat, she was well positioned for a race to the plate if he got a hit. Danny forced himself to focus on the plate.

Ike strung the batter out to a full count. Then, with a 3–2 situation, Drew found the next pitch to his liking and swung at it. It rose high into the air and sailed all the way out to the middle of the center field wall.

That was enough for Tammy. She flew by Danny on her way home.

Bus Thomas, who was playing center for the Bullets for the first time after an injury, was a little slow grabbing the ball. By the time the peg came in to second base, Drew had arrived on the bag standing up.

The Jaguars now had four runs on the scoreboard, and the inning wasn't over. Their fans cheered wildly.

Luckily, Millie Albright, up next, was overeager on the plate. She took three swings in a row and just managed to connect with the last one. It was a pop-up toward first. Joanne snagged it for an easy third out.

As the Bullets came off the field, there wasn't a lot of cheering from their fans. Danny decided to stir things up by shouting, "Okay, you Bullets! Let's show 'em what we can do!"

That got some of the fans and the others members of the team going. But not the first three batters.

Vern went down swinging. Elaine popped one out to third base. Then Frankie Snow, who was playing third base for the Bullets, hit a grounder right into the first baseman's waiting mitt for the final out of the inning.

Coach Lattizori was sticking with Ike. As his team took the field, he called out, "All right, folks, let's see some heads-up ball." If Ike gave away some good pitches, the rest of the team would simply have to make up for it with their field play.

As it happened, Ike gave up mostly bad pitches. Then, on a 3–0 count to the Jaguars' pitcher, Eric Swan, he delivered a meatball down the middle. Eric got under it a little low, and it rose into the air and plopped right into Ike's glove.

With one away, Ike felt more secure and brought down the next two batters with a combination of called strikes and swung-on misses.

This time, as the Bullets came off the field, there was more cheering from the fans. Danny had to laugh when he made out Jennifer's voice crying out, "Let's hear it for a-one and a-two!" Not many in the crowd knew it was his twelfth birthday that very day. Even the guys who were at the party a few days ago seemed to have forgotten.

That was fine with him. He was more interested in getting a piece of the ball when he came up to bat.

Ken was leading off in this second half of the second inning. Danny took his place in the on-deck circle. The second pitch to Ken was low, but Ken liked to scoop the ball sometimes, and he connected solidly. The ball landed deep between center and right field. Al Norris got to it first, but his peg to second was too late. Ken stood on second base and wiped off his brow as the crowd cheered.

This was Danny's chance to keep things going in the right direction for the Bullets. He didn't let them down. He stared down two pitches that broke too late and were called balls. He swung at the next pitch and missed by a mile. Then, with a 2 and 1 count, he got a pitch that was the best birthday present he could have asked for — slightly outside and chest high. This time he swung and connected.

The ball sizzled straight down the hole between short and third. By the time the left fielder had grabbed it, Ken was home and Danny had taken his place on second base.

You could tell how much the crowd liked that from the roar that bellowed forth from the stands. Even Jennifer's voice was lost in all that noise.

All Danny wanted now was to cross the plate. He almost got his chance when Joanne squeaked a grounder by first base for a single. But all he could do was advance one base on it. He was aimed at home plate when Bus Thomas hit a line drive to short, which landed with a *thwap* in Tammy Aiken's glove. Luckily, Danny hadn't tried to run on it. He could see that the Aiken girl was all set to nail him at home with a rocket in that direction.

His itchy feet were held in check when the next batter, Larry, waited out four bad pitches for a walk.

The bases were now loaded, with only one out. With Danny straining at third, Joanne leading off second, and Larry aching to get away from first, Ike came up to bat and struck out. Then Vern's bad luck continued with a grounder to first for an easy third out to end the inning.

The Bullets fans were silent with disappointment. Still, the Bullets had broken onto the scoreboard and were feeling a little better as they took the field.

The Jaguars looked cocky as they came to bat in the top of the third. Then Marsha hit the ball high and deep, but not deep enough. It landed right in the middle of center fielder Bus's glove for the first out.

Ike got a little wild on the mound and bounced a couple of pitches in the dirt, then misfired on two more. That sent Roy Feenie down to first base on a walk.

Tammy Aiken came up to bat for the second time in the game. Again Danny studied her stance — and again he felt a peculiar twinge of recognition, a strange sense of familiarity, when he looked at her crouched at the plate. But this time there was something else about her that bothered him, something he just couldn't quite figure out.

Ike was having a hard time figuring her out, too.

She seemed to be hitting everything he threw her way, even though they were fouls. Then, with an 0 and 2 count, she connected with a solid hit to right field. Fast work by Elaine helped to hold her at first base.

Two for two, thought Danny. And only one out. She's a real scoring threat to us this inning, not to mention this game, the series — and to my standing as the league's leading shortstop! Well, I'll just do everything I can to even things out with Ms. Tammy Aiken.

Danny shifted from foot to foot, trying to concentrate on the play at hand.

Tammy took a long lead off first as Ike wound up for his first pitch to Al Norris. Even though it was slightly out of reach, Al swung at it. It bobbled toward second base, where Vern grabbed it and pegged it to Joanne. She tagged the bag and returned it to him in time for him to squeeze Tammy into a trap for the double play.

Danny breathed a huge sigh of relief.

"Way to go, Bullets!" he shouted as they headed for the dugout.

"Yeah, let's get some hits!" Elaine called out as she

headed for the plate. Leading off that inning, she showed how it was done with a line drive by short that got her on base with a single.

Frankie Snow struck out, but Ken cracked one over the fence for a two-run homer. The fans went wild. The Bullets were now one run short of the Jaguars, who were still leading 4–3.

Danny came up to bat and hoped to even the score — in more ways than one. But Eric seemed to throw him nothing but garbage. Unfortunately, he was so anxious for a hit that he swung at some of it. After popping off about a half dozen foul balls, he swung at something that looked halfway decent and missed altogether.

"Strike three!"

Danny slouched off toward the Bullets' dugout. As he passed Joanne on her way to the plate, she said, "Tough luck, pal. You'll get 'em next time."

But Danny knew that a strikeout looked pretty lame to the critical eyes of the All-Star scouts. And when compared to Tammy's two solid hits, it looked even worse.

Danny didn't bat again that inning, but Joanne walked and Bus sent her home with a double to tie the score. Larry Chuan connected with a line drive down the middle that put him on first. Then, in a heart-stopping play that had the crowd roaring, Bus outran the peg to home. The Bullets were now in the lead, 5–4. Danny cheered with the rest of the team, momentarily forgetting his own disappointment. When Ike popped out to short to end the scoring rally, Danny was all set to keep the Jaguars from a comeback when the coach called him over.

"I want you to take it easy for a while, Danny," he said. "I'm sending Mike in at short for the rest of the game. You know it doesn't mean you haven't done a good job. I just want you in top shape for the remainder of the series. It's going to go at least four and maybe a full five. We're all counting on you, but we have to give everyone a chance to get in some field play as well as hitting."

Danny knew he meant it. The coach had told the team over and over that he was going to shift them around and give as many members of the roster as much playing time as he could.

Still, he felt like a failure, sitting on the bench as the Jaguars came up to bat. He felt even worse as the six hitters who came up to bat managed to knock in two runs before Ike retired the side. As they grabbed their gloves and headed for the field, the Jaguars were now ahead on the scoreboard, 6–5.

Before play began, Danny noticed that Tammy Aiken was lingering on the pitcher's mound. She was talking with Eric Swan and Drew Ferris. He figured they were discussing the next batters who would be coming up for the Bullets. But then he would have sworn that she was pointing toward him. He felt his face turn red.

She's probably laughing at me for sitting on the bench, he thought angrily. Man, she is really starting to bug me!

Danny suddenly started. Tammy had broken into a huge grin — and for a split second, Danny felt as though he was looking into a mirror. The sensation vanished as quickly as it had come, but it left Danny with a pounding heart.

As Tammy took her position at shortstop, Danny found himself studying her more closely than ever.

Whatever had been said on the mound, it sure seemed to have helped Eric. He put down the top of the Bullets' batting order one-two-three to end the inning.

The fifth inning was scoreless for both teams. On the Jaguars' side of the scoreboard, Ike chalked up two strikeouts, and even the mighty Tammy Aiken went hitless. She popped one up to third that Frankie put away easily. When the Bullets came up, Ken and Mike both singled, but Joanne struck out and then Bus hit into a double play.

At the top of the sixth, the Jaguars held on to their one-run lead — but got no further. Ike held them in check by throwing stuff they could barely connect with. Millie flew out to third, Eric struck out, then their last chance, Joey Sands, went down with a grounder to first that Joanne easily put away.

It was the Bullets' last chance at bat. Larry started out with a long fly ball to left. But Wally Mills was right there to put it away.

Then Eric made a big mistake. He walked Ike. The crowd cheered as the Bullets' hard-working southpaw arrived on base for the first time that game.

The next batter, Vern Labar, hit one deep into center field that bounced off the wall before it could be stopped. It was enough to send Ike home. It also put a runner on second base with only one out.

The score was now tied 6–6. The crowd roared as Elaine came up to bat.

"Go, Elaine, go!"

"We want a hit!"

"All the way, Elaine!"

The umpire signaled for the crowd to quiet down, and the noise stopped.

Elaine choked up and stepped in for the first pitch.

"Steeeee-rike!" called the ump.

Elaine barely moved. She just waited for the next pitch.

It came. She swung. She hit the ball.

The round white ball with the tiny stitches sky-rocketed into deep right field just inside the foul pole. It was a fair ball. Elaine took off for first, and Vern's legs tore up the track as he raced for home. It was no contest. He was jumping up and screaming before the ball got close to the catcher's mitt.

The whole team went wild. The Bullets had pulled off a victory, 7–6, at the very last moment!

There was a lot of celebrating in their dugout as they all slapped high fives and tens on one another.

Then, suddenly, Danny heard singing on the other side of the field. It came from the Jaguars' dugout.

Above the noise of the Bullets' celebration, he could just make out what they were singing: "Happy birthday to you, happy birthday, dear *Tammmm-mmy . . .*"

Danny stood stock still as the final words of the song floated across the field. His mind was awhirl with confusion.

"Looks like you two have something else in common," a voice behind him commented. It was Joel. For once, he didn't look like he was joking around.

"Yeah," Danny said weakly. "Weird, huh?"

He thought about the discovery he'd made about Tammy in the library the day before, and the strange feeling he'd been having all game — that Tammy was somehow *familiar* to him.

"Yeah," he repeated slowly. "And I don't think that's the half of it."

7

Danny found the house empty when he arrived home. But he knew there would be a small family dinner to celebrate his birthday that evening. Mrs. Walker had promised to make his favorite, Hawaiian pork chops with extra pineapple. She was probably out shopping.

The excitement of the game and the confusing thoughts bouncing around in his head had left him exhausted. He didn't feel like doing anything but flopping down in front of the TV. He was in the mood for something really mindless, like an old horror flick or a cowboy movie. Anything but baseball.

He clicked the TV on, then headed for the couch, where he stretched out. A talk show lady appeared on the screen, blabbing away. Danny searched for the remote control, but it was nowhere in sight. He was just about to get up when something the woman said caught his attention.

"It's not that difficult to find out who your parents are if you're adopted. You may even have relatives you never dreamed you had!"

Danny sat bolt upright, his heart pounding.

"Just call this number" — an 800 telephone number was flashed on the TV screen. It was recorded instantly in his brain — "for an application that will set the wheels in motion. In no time at all, you could be on your way to knowing who your family really is."

Danny got up from the couch and turned off the TV.

Am I going crazy, or could what I'm thinking about Tammy and me possibly be true? he thought wonderingly. I guess there's just one way to find out.

He went to the telephone and dialed the 800 number.

The morning after his birthday, Danny lay awake in bed, staring at the ceiling and thinking about the phone call he'd made the day before.

The man who had answered the phone had taken

down Danny's name and address, but that was all. He'd told Danny to keep an eye on the mail for a packet of information. The whole call had taken less than a minute.

So why do I feel so *guilty*? Danny thought miserably.

But he was pretty sure he knew the answer. He'd known all his life that he was adopted. His parents had been very open and honest with him about it. He knew that his biological mother had died in a car crash when he'd been born and that his biological grandparents had not been able to take on the burden of raising a newborn. He'd never given such matters a second thought, except to be grateful that his adoptive parents loved him like he was their own son. The last thing he'd want would be to hurt them in any way.

By seeking information about how to trace his biological roots, he knew he was risking doing just that. But the events of the last few days — ending with the bizarre coincidence of Tammy sharing his birthday — had made him more than curious. He wasn't ready to tell anyone his suspicions just yet, though. He wanted to get proof.

Proof that he and Tammy had more in common than playing shortstop.

A lot more.

During the next few days, Danny worked like a demon around the house and garden. He always seemed to be there right when the mail carrier came, too.

"What did you send away for?" asked Jennifer, grabbing some magazines from him the morning of the third game in the series. "A magic decoder ring?"

"Don't be funny," he said. "This is serious. I'm waiting for some very important information to get here."

"Oh, an application?" she asked.

He blanched. His jaw dropped. How could she have known? Had she been listening in on the extension upstairs when he called the 800 number? He was about to accuse her of eavesdropping — which was totally forbidden in the Walker household — when she finished her question.

"For college?" she went on. "Why don't you wait until after the series. Maybe you'll have something special to put down. I don't even want to say the words that come after *county*, 'cause I don't want to jinx you. Especially before today's game."

"Hey, thanks a lot," Danny said. He gave her a friendly tap on her shoulder. "You're okay, you know?" He dumped the mail on the little desk in the front hall.

Brinnnng!

The telephone rang, and Jennifer flew off upstairs to answer it.

"It's probably for me!" she called behind.

Her quick departure knocked the letters off the desk. When Danny stooped to pick them up, he saw that he had missed one addressed to him. It looked just like those sweepstakes letters his folks always got, with a fancy border all around the envelope. But there was his name right on the address label.

He ripped it open and read the letter on top of the application form.

Dear Mr. Walker
   Thank you for your inquiry . . .

The letter was long and there were a lot of sentences that didn't half make sense. But down near the bottom he came to the bad news.

To cover the cost of servicing your application, we require an initial deposit of $100. This will be credited against the final cost of our investigation.

A hundred dollars! And that's just to start! There was no way he could come up with anywhere near that amount.

"Aren't you getting ready for the game?" his mother called out to him from the back of the house.

"Yes!" he answered quickly. He shoved the letter into his back pocket and ran upstairs.

He changed as fast as he could, carelessly dumping his clothes in a heap on the floor as he pulled on his uniform. At the last second, he remembered the roll of film he'd shot at the previous game. He grabbed it out of his camera and headed back downstairs.

"Hey, Mom!" he called. "Could you drop this film off for me?"

"Sure," his mother answered. "And Danny, I'm sorry I haven't been able to make any of your games. I've just been too busy at work to get away."

It seemed to Danny that she was about to say something else. But instead, she dug her car keys out of her pocketbook and unlocked the car door.

A few minutes later, Danny was warming up on the field with the rest of the team.

"Danny, you're back at short," Coach Lattizori announced when he called the team together. "We'll go with the same lineup as the first game. I took a look at the Jaguars' roster. They're doing the same thing. Okay, folks, let's see some real good baseball out there now."

The third game began. Both teams played well during the first inning. The Bullets batted first and managed to hit some pitches. But only one of them ended up in fair territory for a hit. With a runner on base, Ken popped one up that the pitcher, Andy Hooten, caught to retire the Bullets.

When the Jaguars were at bat, Marc gave up one walk, but he struck out the next batter. Then Marsha Kerns almost hit into a double play with a line drive to second base. But Vern's peg to Danny, who was covering second, wasn't quick enough. The runner advanced. Then, to shatter the Jaguars' hopes of scoring that inning, Roy Feenie struck out.

Danny led off for the Bullets at the top of the second. As he stepped into the batter's box, he felt pretty good. Then he stared down the line toward the pitcher's mound. In the corner of his eye he could see Tammy settling down, crouching, waiting for the play.

"Strike!"

That brought him back to the game real fast. He hadn't even seen that pitch.

But he did get a fix on the next one — and a piece of it with his bat. The ball sailed into center field and in a matter of seconds, he was on base with a clean single. It felt good to get a hit first time at bat.

Standing on the bag while the next batter got set, he glanced across the field. This time he couldn't help but see Tammy. She had taken off her cap and was tugging at her ponytail, sort of pushing it out of the way. But she was staring straight across the field — at him. And she was scowling. It was the kind of look he'd seen on linemen in football games when the TV showed a close-up — real mean and unfriendly.

Maybe she's just angry that I got the game's first hit, he thought. Or maybe something else is bothering her.

He didn't have a lot of time to dwell on that question. The crack of the bat set him off to second base, where he arrived safely despite a good catch by the Jaguars' right fielder for the first out.

Andy Hooten recovered his stuff and struck out the next two Bullets batters. That ended Danny's chance for scoring that inning.

At the top of the third, the Jaguars went down one-two-three in what turned out to be one of the quickest innings of the series. One strikeout, one pop fly, and one foul ball caught by the third baseman. According to the scorebook, Marc had thrown only seven pitches! Danny hadn't even had to wipe off his forehead.

"Nice going, Marc," said Danny, coming off the field. He caught himself before he said anything else. Marc was working on a shutout, and he didn't want to jinx it.

Gee, he thought, I'm as superstitious as Jennifer. I guess it runs in the family. That started the old brain machinery going. Family. What did it mean? He and Jennifer were both adopted. But the Walkers were one of the closest, most loving families in town. Sure, they fought once in a while, but they were a family. That meant everything to him. So why was he sniffing around outside of it, looking for information about someone he'd never even officially *met*?

While Danny mulled this over, Marc started off the inning by striking out. Then the top of the Bullets' batting order came up to the plate. Vern got the fans on their feet with a line drive between short and third that turned into a single. Then Elaine's powerful swing sent one deep into center. Vern advanced easily to third, and Elaine stood up safely at second.

With only one out, the chances of scoring during that inning looked pretty good. Mike was up at bat next, and Danny knew he was capable of the big one.

But the Jaguars' pitcher knew that, too. He kept the ball so far away from Mike that the Bullets' third baseman ended up jogging down to first on a walk. The bases were now loaded.

That brought Ken up. He had yet to connect with the ball this game. Unfortunately that record held. Ken went down swinging for the second Bullets out. Danny came up to bat.

This was his big chance. Two away. Bases loaded. Nothing but goose eggs on the scoreboard for both teams.

"Just a hit, Danny," Coach Lattizori had said when he grabbed his batting helmet. "That's all you have to do. Go out there, relax, and let your instincts take over. You're a natural, and you'll find yourself a nice piece of the ball."

That wasn't enough. He was sure that the red-headed shortstop was glaring across the infield at him. He'd show her. He'd come up with the big one. He could practically taste it.

Danny rubbed his toe in the dirt, then settled in to the batter's box.

The Jaguars' pitcher released a fastball. Danny swung hard — but just barely connected. The ball went foul.

The next pitch was a repeat of the first. So was Danny's hit. With the count now at 0 and 2, Danny could feel the tension getting to him. He stepped quickly out of the batter's box.

He tried not to even hear the shouting from the stands as the Bullets fans clamored for a hit.

Instead he scanned the field. Everyone was in position. There were playing him deep. They expected him to go for the big one. That's what he wanted. All he had to do was hit the ball squarely with the piece of wood he held in his tight grip. Forget about that blur between second and third with a glint of auburn hair. Don't even think about her, he said to himself as he stepped back into the box.

Whoosh!

He caught the pitcher's motion out of the corner of his eye. Instinctively, he swung. And this time, he connected solidly.

But it wasn't enough. With a perfectly timed leap into the air, Tammy Aiken caught his hard-hit ball for the third out.

The others on the team tried to hide their disappointment.

"That was an unbelievable catch," said Joel. "Just like you would have done, Danny."

"Just don't let it get you down. You'll get another shot," said Joanne.

Yeah, but would it happen this game? Would the coach take him out?

"Danny," the coach called before he could dash out to the diamond.

Uh-oh, this is it, he thought. He's giving me the bad news.

"Danny," Coach Lattizori said, "you're playing

Millie a little too deep. She hasn't been hitting that strong, and I think you ought to come in on her a little. Now go out there and do your stuff."

That's it? That's all? The coach was keeping him in? Danny realized he'd been holding his breath. He let it out with a *whoosh*.

As he went off to take his position on the field, he was filled with a new determination. Okay, I might not have done it at bat, he said to himself, but they're not getting anything by me on the field.

He lived up to his promise. For the rest of the game, he concentrated on every play. His fielding was top quality. At bat, he walked once and got on base once. He even managed to score by outrunning a peg to home. It turned out to be the Bullets' only run of the game.

The Jaguars made it onto the scoreboard as well — with a power-drive homerun hit from their number-one slugger, her red ponytail streaming behind her as she ran across the plate.

The score was still tied, 1–1, at the bottom of the sixth. Tammy was on first when Drew Ferris, their hard-hitting catcher, came up to bat.

The count was 2 and 2 when Drew found the pitch he wanted.

Crack!

The ball sailed high into the sky above center field. It looked like it was going all the way. Tammy took off from first. Danny didn't even want to see her as she started to round second toward the winning run.

But the ball dropped, hit the end of the center field fence, and bounced inside. Joel was on top of it in an instant. He threw it wildly in the direction of the plate but only got it as far as the infield. Danny was the closest. He scooped it up, whirled around, and as Tammy approached the plate, he pegged it home.

Larry grabbed it and twisted for the touch, but Tammy had just slid under him and scored.

The Jaguars had just won game three, 2–1. And that's the way the series stood as well: 2–1 in their favor.

The morning after the third game, Joel swung by the Walker house right after breakfast. Danny was still sitting at the table after everyone else had gone off. He was pushing a spoon around his cereal bowl and staring at the lines it made in the thin film of milk at the bottom.

"Yo, slugger, how's it going?" Joel asked.

"Slugger, hah!" Danny muttered.

Joel grabbed a chair, twisted it around, straddled it, and sat down.

"Yup, just what Dr. Joel figured. The patient is in a rotten mood. As part of the team that is now one down in a crucial series, the patient is cracking up," he said.

"Very funny, Joel," said Danny. "Don't start in on one of those Dr. Joel routines."

The two boys had grown up in the same neighborhood and had known each other forever. All the Jackson kids went to the same school as the Walkers, and they had started out playing in the same sandboxes. Danny and Joel had been best friends for years.

When they were in second grade, Joel had gotten a doctor kit as a Christmas present, and he took it very seriously. For a while, Danny had gone along as his "patient" and let Joel wrap long strips of gauze around his head and slap bandages all over his arms.

The doctor kit got put aside when Joel discovered other kinds of medicine. For the last year or so, he had decided that he might become a psychiatrist. So now he walked around spouting words that he thought might come from a shrink.

Luckily he had a sense of humor about it. He didn't mind when Danny and the others ribbed him about his doctoring. Joel could take it as well as dish it out.

"Zo, Danny," said Joel, putting on a fake accent, "if you don't vant to come to ze doctor, zen ze doctor has to come to you. My prescription for zis ailment of ze brain is fresh air and exercise."

"Oh, great," said Danny, laughing despite himself. "Very original. What would you have said if it'd been raining right now?"

Joel shook his head. "Vell, it isn't, so don't get smart viz ze doctor." He grinned. "Get cleaned up and shake a leg. I've got my bike outside. Let's go for a ride over to the mall and see if the new *Dagger of Death* video is in. We can watch it later on — if it does rain. Or tonight after dinner. What do you say?"

"Might as well," Danny answered.

"Come on," said Joel. He pointed at the table. "Though first, you'd better clean up that mess you made. Hey, you weren't just —"

"No, I wasn't crying over *spilled milk,* Doctor!" said Danny. He threw a dish towel at Joel and ran out the door.

On the ride over to the mall, Joel tried to keep Danny from mulling over the game.

"It wasn't an error," he said, referring to Danny's throw to home. "You didn't waste any time. Neither did I. It was a great hit and a terrific run. Nothing anyone could do about it."

"If only I had —" Danny started to say for the zillionth time.

"If only you don't knock it off, Dr. Joel will have to pay you another visit!" Joel shouted.

They parked their bikes and locked them in the rack outside the mall entrance. When they got inside, they went right to the video store. They headed for the section marked "New Arrivals."

They scanned the shelves, then went back and checked more carefully — no *Dagger of Death*.

"Rats!" said Joel. "I really wanted to see it."

"Well, pick something else," said Danny. "Maybe we ought to get something funny instead."

"You don't think *Dagger of Death* would be a million laughs?" asked Joel.

"Come on," said Danny. He dragged his friend over to the "Comedy" display. They picked two videos, one they'd seen years ago and a brand-new one that neither of them had seen before.

"They ought to be good for a few laughs later on," said Joel.

They left the video store and started walking down the main strip inside the mall when Danny saw the photo shop.

"Hey, wait a minute," he said. "My mom dropped off some film for me the other day. It might be ready."

"You want to pick it up?" asked Joel.

"Yeah, I'll save her the trip," said Danny.

The Walker photos had come back. Danny paid for them, and the clerk handed him the package.

"Let's see what they look like," said Joel when they got outside.

"Maybe later," said Danny evasively. "Right now I'm starving. Come on, I'll race you to the bike rack." He shoved the photo package in his shirt pocket and ran off. Joel came tearing after him, and they both touched the rack at the same time. "Tie!" they yelled, and exchanged high fives. They put on their helmets and headed home.

As they got near the Walker house, Joel looked at his watch. "I'd better get home. Give me a call later, and we'll figure out when we're going to watch these videos, okay?"

"Okay," said Danny. He put his bike in the garage and went inside the house. Mrs. Walker was in the bathroom sorting laundry.

"Hi, Mom," said Danny. "Need any help?"

"No, I'm fine," she said. "Thanks."

"Okay," he said, and went off to his bedroom.

Danny hadn't lied to Joel. He was hungry, but that

could wait. Right now, his instincts told him to examine his pictures without anyone looking over his shoulder.

When he opened the photo pack, he was glad he'd followed his gut feeling. He flipped through the pictures till he came to the last one: the close-up he'd taken of Tammy Aiken. The minute he saw the photo, he knew that what he'd been thinking could be true.

She looks *exactly* like me, he thought. And I bet I know someone who would agree — someone who's been holding back important information from me for a long time!

He grabbed the pile of photos and went back into the kitchen.

"Hey, Mom," he said, "I want you to take a look at something."

Mrs. Walker turned toward him, shoving something in her pants pocket as she did. Danny noticed that she looked a little odd, but he shrugged it off.

"What is it, Danny?" she asked.

"Take a look," he said. He quickly shuffled all the pictures, then laid them out on the kitchen table.

Mrs. Walker sat down and put on her glasses.

"That's a nice one of Elaine and Joanne. And that Joel — always the comedian. Jennifer looks —" she stopped suddenly and picked up the close-up of Tammy Aiken. She gasped and bit her lip, then took off her glasses.

Danny thought she was going to break into tears at any second.

"I'm not just imagining it, am I, Mom?" he asked quietly. "This girl looks like me. And I think you know something about it, but you're not telling me. Why? *What is it about this girl?*"

The anguish in his voice cried out for an answer. There was no mistaking that.

Mrs. Walker covered her face for a moment, then quickly wiped away the tears that had gushed over at his plea for information. She got up from the table and started for the living room.

"Come with me, Danny," she said. "I have something you'd better see for yourself."

She went to her desk and took out a small wooden box with a tiny brass lock. Danny and Jennifer knew the box was there, but they'd thought it had money inside. Mrs. Walker sometimes mentioned the "mad money" she had hidden away in case of emergencies, and they figured that was where she kept it.

When she unlocked the box, however, Danny saw that there was no money inside. Instead it was filled with newspaper clippings. Danny could see one that he remembered from the headline: "Danny Walker Wins Little League MVP."

Mrs. Walker rummaged through the box and took out a yellowed newspaper clipping from the bottom.

"You'd better read this," she said.

Danny took the clipping and sat down.

He read the story of a terrible accident. A young woman about to give birth was on the way to the hospital with her husband when their car was struck by a speeding pickup truck. The husband died instantly, but the young woman was rushed to the emergency room, where she died shortly after giving birth — to twins, a boy and a girl. The date of the tragedy was the same day as Danny's birthday.

There was a picture of the young woman, taken before the accident. She could have been Danny's older sister. In fact, she looked a lot like an older version of Tammy Aiken.

9

Danny could hardly believe his eyes. There was no question about the resemblance among the woman, Tammy — and himself.

"Yes, Danny," said Mrs. Walker. "That's a picture of your biological mother."

"And . . . and . . . Tammy?" he asked. "She looks just like Tammy."

"Tammy is the other twin she gave birth to before she died," Mrs. Walker said.

"But I never knew I had a twin sister," he blurted out. "Why not? Why didn't anyone ever tell me? Is there something wrong with her? With me? I just don't understand."

"Oh, Danny, there's nothing wrong with either of you," said Mrs. Walker. "You were both beautiful, healthy, wonderful babies when you were born.

And you're just as wonderful now — and I'm sure Tammy is, too. I'll explain everything if you'll just calm down.

"Let's go into the kitchen, and I'll make us both some lemonade."

Danny wasn't sure he could get anything down his throat, but he followed her anyway. He took the yellowed newspaper clipping with him and stared at it again. He just couldn't get over how much the picture looked like Tammy grown up a little.

When the lemonade was ready, Mrs. Walker poured two glasses. She dropped an ice cube in Danny's glass and sat down.

"Your dad and I argued endlessly about how to tell you that you had a twin sister," she started to explain. "We just couldn't agree on when the right time would be. Then, as you grew older, we just kept putting it off.

"So you can imagine how I felt when I found *this* in your pocket a moment ago." She held out a crumpled piece of paper. Danny recognized the letter and application form he had called for.

"Mom, let me explain —" he started to say.

Mrs. Walker held up her hand. "There's no need,

Danny. I know you were simply following your instincts to figure out something you should have learned from your father and me a long time ago. And we were going to tell you, right after the championship. We were afraid that if you found out before, it would affect your playing. We had no idea you suspected something." She shook her head.

"Why couldn't you tell me?" he asked. "What's so horrible about having a twin sister?"

"Oh, no, Danny, there's nothing bad about that," she said, patting his arm. "We were afraid you'd think we were terrible for separating the two of you. But we had no choice."

"Why didn't you just adopt both of us?" he asked.

"We would have loved to," she said. "But that wasn't really possible for a number of reasons. First of all, Tammy was spoken for. You see, we had registered with the hospital's adoption service. So had the Aikens, but they were ahead of us. They were notified that a little girl had been born and came to claim her when they discovered there were twins."

"So, the Aikens could have adopted both of us?" he asked.

"Not really," she said. "They were young and

couldn't afford to have two children. And we already had Jennifer, who was only two years old. Your father had just started his own business, and we couldn't afford all three of you. So we were each given a wonderful gift, someone to treasure forever."

Danny couldn't even hold the lemonade glass. He just stared at the table as Mrs. Walker continued.

"The Aikens lived over on the west side of town back then," she said. "We didn't see each other except when we bumped into each other at a restaurant or a movie once in a while. In fact, I never saw Tammy after they left the hospital with her. But we did keep in touch, at first by phone, and then we wrote when they moved out to the coast. And then the letters slowed down and turned into once-a-year Christmas cards. And then, eventually, that stopped, too. There really wasn't much that we seemed to be able to say to each other."

"So you lost touch with my twin sister?" Danny asked in disbelief.

"I'm afraid so," said his mother quietly. "But we never really thought about her that way. We felt that we had created a family among ourselves — you and

Jennifer, Dad and I. Tammy hadn't even crossed my mind in years until you said her name the other day. I was shocked to hear that the Aikens had moved back this way."

"They actually don't live here," he said. "They live in Jamestown."

"It's close by," said Mrs. Walker. "I'm sure they would have been in touch with us sooner or later. Oh, I wish I'd found out before you did, Danny. You know your father and I would never do anything to hurt you."

At that, Danny looked up. Tears were filling her eyes. There were deep wrinkles on her forehead, and she was rubbing her hands together over and over. He felt numb, but he could tell his mother was in terrible pain.

Danny got up from his seat and went over to her. He bent down and threw his arms around her and buried his face next to her cheek.

"I love you, Mom," he said. "I know you didn't do anything bad on purpose. Neither did Dad. You just couldn't."

"Oh, Danny," she sighed, and let her tears flow.

"I'm just glad I finally know what's been going on," he said. "And I want to think about it."

He kissed her. Then he went off to his room and shut the door behind him.

For a long time, the Walker house was very quiet. No sounds came from Danny's room, where he lay on the bed and stared at the ceiling. A million thoughts raced around in his head, but none of them came in for a landing.

Finally there was a tap on the door. Before he could even tell someone to come in or stay away, Jennifer announced, "It's me, and I have food."

Danny realized that he hadn't eaten anything since breakfast, and he was hungry. He could almost hear his stomach growling at the mention of the word *food*. Still, he was a little nervous about talking to anyone about what he'd just found out.

He stalled. "Anything good?" he asked.

"Bologna and Swiss on rye with mustard and mayo and a half-sour pickle sliced in quarters," she announced. "That good enough for you?"

The sound of her voice, with its slightly exasperated tone, was so familiar that Danny suddenly felt a whole lot better. No matter what had happened in the past or what might happen in the days to come, he knew who his family was. Nothing was ever going to change that.

"Okay, come on," he called, sitting up on the edge of his bed.

Jennifer entered, handed him the plate with his sandwich, and flopped down in the chair next to his bedroom window.

"So, what do you think?" she asked.

Good old Jennifer, he said to himself with a smile. She doesn't beat around the bush.

"Mom sent you to find out how I was?" he asked.

"Of course," she answered. "She told me the whole story, too. Wow, I never even guessed. I thought you had a little bit of a crush on that Aiken girl. You sure didn't hide your interest."

"Get off it," he said. "I just couldn't figure out why she looked like someone I knew. It wasn't until I saw her picture that it all really clicked. I mean, a twin sister. It sounds so weird."

They were quiet for a moment, thinking their own thoughts. Then Jennifer cleared her throat.

"So, now that you know, I suppose you'll be trading me in, then?" Jennifer suggested. She said it jokingly, but she didn't look at him.

Danny started to laugh. "Not unless she washes and dries the dishes, takes out the garbage, makes my bed, and carries my lunch to school," Danny said, munching on the last of the sandwich.

"Be my guest," said Jennifer with a wide grin. "Good luck to the two of you!"

Danny threw a pillow in her direction but missed.

"Relax," he said. "You're stuck with me. Besides, Tammy doesn't even know about me. I mean, I don't think so. Did Mom say anything about that to you?"

"No, she said she and Dad haven't even spoken to the Aikens since they moved back," said Jennifer, picking up the pillow and plumping it in her lap.

"So Tammy probably doesn't know," said Danny. "Or maybe she does. But I don't *know* if she knows, and she doesn't know if *I* know." He sighed. "Boy, is this complicated."

He shook his head, trying to clear up the thoughts that kept bouncing around.

"What do you think?" he asked. "If I find out she doesn't know, should I tell her?"

Jennifer shook her head. Danny knew there was no way she could come up with an answer to his question. "You're on your own there, slugger," she said. "I think you'll just have to play it by ear."

The word *slugger* reminded him: He'd be seeing Tammy the next day, at the fourth game in the championship series.

"Come on, let's play some Wiffle ball in the backyard," he said. "Gotta keep in shape for the game."

Jennifer followed him out, and for the next hour or so they caroused around the yard, chasing the white plastic ball, which never went very far.

While waiting for Jennifer to shag a hit, Danny noticed his mother looking out the window. A moment later, his father appeared at her side and put his arm around her shoulders. Danny smiled, knowing everything was going to be all right.

At least with *his* family.

The next day, Danny got to the field early. He'd left his camera at home this time because all he wanted to do now was play baseball. Besides, it wasn't too late to show what he could do on the diamond. He still had a chance at being picked for the county All-Stars. All he had to do was play his best. It was up to the whole team to see that the Jaguars didn't win this one to end the series as the champs.

Danny had decided to keep the fact that Tammy was his twin sister from his teammates. So far he hadn't said anything to anyone about it — not even Joel. The Walkers had agreed at dinner to let him decide for himself how he wanted to handle it. Jennifer was sworn to secrecy. She didn't have to lie. She just had to keep her mouth shut about Danny and Tammy.

But she wasn't keeping her mouth shut about her favorite baseball team.

"Come on, you Bullets!" she shouted from the stands. "You can do it!"

Danny gave her a big smile as he jogged to his spot at short. Then he crouched down to wait for the first pitch. Ike Isaacs was on the mound for the Bullets, facing Joey Sands, the Jaguars' usual lead-off batter.

Ike started things off strong with a strikeout. But he followed it up by walking Wally Mills.

Marsha got under an outside pitch and hit a high one. Wally advanced to second before Danny pulled the ball in for the second out.

Then Ray grounded out to first to end the inning for the Jaguars, with no score yet on the board.

Before the Bullets took their turn in the batter's box, Coach Lattizori called them into a circle outside their dugout.

"I don't have to tell you," he said. "There's a lot riding on this game. But don't let that get in your way. Remember what you've learned all season, and use it. If we play hard and smart, we can tie this series up. And who knows? Some of you may get a chance to play for the All-Stars. But for now, let's get out there and show them some hitting."

The team took him at his word. The coach had juggled things around a little for this game so that Mike Worsley would lead off. He'd be followed by

Bus Thomas, who was playing right field. Frankie Snow, at third base this game, would be the number-three batter. Ken, who was playing left field, was in the cleanup slot. Danny was in his usual fifth slot, followed by Joanne, then center fielder Joel. Larry and Ike rounded off the batting order.

Mike let a couple of real low pitches go by before he found one he liked. He belted it out to short left field for a two-bagger.

Bus came up next. He swung hard at the first pitch, which was much too high. The next one was a called strike. Then, with an 0 and 2 count, he connected with a line drive between second and third. Millie was a bit slow grabbing it, and her throw home was too late. Mike scored the first run of the game, and Bus held on second.

Eric Swan, the Jaguars' ace southpaw, threw two strikes on Frankie before he started to unravel. The next three pitches were all way outside.

"Good eyes, Frankie," shouted Danny from the dugout. "How to watch 'em, buddy!"

The next pitch nearly grazed Frankie's ankles. He dropped his bat for the trip to first, and Ken came up to bat.

With runners on first and second, Ken was a real threat. But to the Jaguars' great relief, he tipped a half dozen foul balls. Then he struck out.

With only one out, Danny stepped into the batter's box. He couldn't help noticing that the Jaguars' outfield backed up a little. It felt good to see them playing him deep.

But he surprised them with a line drive down the third base line. It looked like it might curve and fall outside the marker, but it didn't. It was just enough to make Joey Sands, the Jaguars' third baseman, chase it before he could stop the ball. By the time Joey was ready to throw, Bus had crossed the plate. Danny had started for second, but wisely beat it back to first before Roy could tap him out.

"C'mon, Joanne!" Danny yelled. "Send Frankie and me home!" But his hopes of scoring ended when first Joanne and then Joel popped out to short.

As he jogged in from first base, Danny couldn't help thinking how nice those two outs would look to the All-Star scouts. Two outs in a row proved that Tammy's playing was consistent — and that she didn't crack under pressure.

Wonder if she'd act as cool if she knew the truth

about us, he thought. But just as quickly, he pushed the thought away. We may be alike on the surface, but that could be where the similarity ends. I'll find a way to tell her — but not until *after* the series is over.

Tammy was the leadoff hitter for the Jaguars in the second inning. Danny shifted from foot to foot as Tammy approached the plate. He tried to keep calm as she let the first pitch, a beauty, go by for a called strike. And then —

Crack!

He tried not to feel his heart race as he watched the ball soar into the air and then drop out of sight behind the right field fence.

A home run! She jogged round the bases without any expression on her face until she reached the plate. But she broke out in a big smile before she joined her team in their dugout.

"She's some hot stuff, that shortstop," said Mike from third base.

"Game's not over," mumbled Danny.

She's just another player. She's just another player. He'd thought that if he kept saying it to himself, he'd be able to concentrate on his own game.

After Tammy's homer, Ike settled down and

retired the next three Jaguar hitters to end the top of the second. The score now read Bullets 2, Jaguars 1.

The Bullets came in and took their shot at putting some more runs on the scoreboard. But they had a dismal inning. Larry was thrown out at first, Ike struck out, and then Mike hit one into the waiting glove of the Jaguars' second baseman.

Eric Swan, the Jaguars' first batter at the top of the third, hadn't had a hit all series. He did pretty much what everyone expected of him. He struck out.

Then came the top of the Jaguars' batting order. Joey Sands approached the plate with a serious look on his face. He seemed determined to get a hit. And he did. It was a clean single to short right field, a solid hit.

Wally Mills hit the ball deep into center field to put himself on base. A quick peg by Joel kept Joey on second.

"C'mon, let's put 'em away!" Danny cried. The team took up the chatter as Marsha came up to the plate. But the chatter died when Ike gave up a walk. The bases were now loaded. The Jaguars' fans were screaming for a hit and some scoring.

Roy Feenie was the next batter. He let the count go to 3 and 1 before he took a swing. And then he hit the ball into the waiting glove of Frankie Snow. Joey Sands managed to slide back just in time to avoid the tag.

With bases still loaded, Tammy came up to bat.

Just another batter, just another batter, said Danny to himself. But in the back of his mind, he could just imagine what would happen to his chances of being picked county All-Star shortstop if she hit a grand-slam homer right now. How would he feel about that?

He never got a chance to find out. Tammy let two called strikes go by her before she swung and missed for the third out. With three runners left on base, the Jaguars went scoreless that inning.

The Bullets didn't do much better. Bus got a single by putting it between short and second. But Frankie grounded out, and then Ken hit a pop fly ball that the pitcher relayed to first, catching Bus off base for a double play. The inning ended with the score still Bullets 2, Jaguars 1.

The game picked up some steam in the fourth inning. Al Norris started things going for the Jaguars with a line drive deep into right field. It took him to second base without much trouble. Millie came up next and drove him home with a sweet single into center that Joel had to run in to grab. Despite a terrific throw home, Al scored to tie the game 2 – 2.

With Millie on first, Drew came up and found the sweet spot on one of Ike's breaking pitches. He connected for a solid hit that took Millie to third while he stayed on first. And there were still no outs for the Jaguars in the inning.

Eric came up to bat and the field came in a little. He woofed the first two pitches, but to everyone's surprise, connected with the ball on the third. It sizzled toward short, but Danny was ready. He leapt, caught the ball in the air for the out, then whirled and pegged it to third. Frankie caught the ball and darted around in time to tag Millie for the double play.

The crowd roared its approval. Danny felt the blood rushing through his veins for the first time in a long while.

Joey Sands struck out to kill the Jaguars' chances for another score that inning, and the Bullets came off the field.

"What a guy! What a guy! Mr. Double Play!"

shouted Joel, coming in from center field. When he caught up with Danny, he slapped him a high five with his ungloved hand.

"Easy there," said Danny. "I'm up at bat now."

"I tell you, there's just no rest for you superstars," said Joel with a big smile on his face. Danny knew his buddy was really pleased that he'd had a good inning out on the field. Now it was time to get the Bullets going in the hitting department.

He did just that. He went to a 3 and 0 count before he found the pitch he was waiting for, but then he walloped the ball. It soared into deep left field and hit the fence before it bounced hard toward the center of the outfield.

With his legs pumping for all they were worth, Danny sped around the bases as the Jaguars' outfield scrambled for the ball. Center fielder Al Norris finally stopped it in time to throw to third. But Danny managed to slide under the peg and touch the base safely before he was tagged. It was a nice, clean triple.

Now, *that* should help, Danny thought as he dusted off his pants. Both the team *and* my stats!

Joanne helped her stats, too, with a solid hit.

Danny crossed the plate at the same time she landed on second with a double. The score was now Bullets 3–Jaguars 2.

Things slowed down a little when Joel Jackson, up at bat next, took three called strikes.

"Tough luck, buddy," said Danny. "Plenty more chances, though. You'll show 'em."

With one away, Eric gave up a walk to Larry Chuan. Then Ike came up to bat. Danny could hardly believe it when the Bullets' pitcher clobbered the ball deep into right field. It was enough to bring Joanne home. Larry wisely stopped at second. Ike was out at first, but he was a happy guy as he flopped down on the bench. The Bullets' lead had increased to two runs.

"An RBI for Ike," said Frankie. "Dynamite!"

Up at bat next, Mike tapped a ground ball that hit the mound and bounced off toward third. Joey stopped it and threw it to second, but he was too late to catch Larry. Larry held where he was as Mike stood up on first.

Then Bus Thomas socked a line drive straight into Tammy's mitt to end the inning. The score was Bullets 4–Jaguars 2.

In the fifth inning, the Jaguars put two players on base before their first out. Then Ike walked Tammy before striking out the next two batters. It looked as though the Jaguars were starting to run out of steam.

The Bullets, however, were just getting started. Frankie walked, Ken struck out for the second time in the game, but Danny got a clean stand-up double by hitting the ball deep into right field. It was enough to send Frankie home. The Bullets' score went to 5 runs against the Jaguars' 2.

Then Joanne popped one up to short for the second out. Tammy spun to toss the ball to the second baseman for the double play, but Danny wasn't taking chances and had stayed right where he was. Their eyes met briefly, then Tammy turned and threw the ball back to the pitcher.

Joel came up and got his first hit of the game. He arrived safely on first, and Danny held up at third. With two men on base, the Bullets stood a chance of scoring another run. But it didn't happen. Larry struck out to end the fifth inning with the Bullets three runs up on the Jaguars.

As Danny ran off to his field position, he felt good. He'd hit a single, a double, and a triple all in the same game. That didn't happen often. Even if he didn't get up to bat again, his series average was looking good.

But the Bullets still had their work cut out for them. They could end the game if they contained the Jaguars in the top of the sixth inning.

Drew Ferris led off. He put one by Mike to arrive safe on first. Next up was Eric, but the Jaguars put in a pinch hitter for him. Barney Gold, their substitute outfielder, came up and faced Ike. The Bullets' outfield played him deep.

The first two pitches were low and inside, and Barney let them go by. The next two were down the middle for called strikes. He swung at the fifth pitch and connected. It was a high fly ball into center field, and Joel was ready for it. He put it away for the first out and pegged the ball to third. Drew held up at second.

The shouting from the Bullets' fans began in the stands: "We want a win! We want a win!"

The ump signaled for them to quiet down.

Next up was Joey Sands. Ike walked him. There were runners on first and second.

Wally Mills stepped into the batter's box and took

a few practice swings. He settled down to try for a hit, but Ike walked him, too. The bases were now loaded with only one out.

Danny could feel the tension all around him. His own heart was pounding madly. Got to remain cool, he thought. He took a deep breath and settled down for the next pitch.

Marsha let the first two go by for a 1 and 1 count. The next one started to break in the direction she liked, and she went for it. She connected with a ground ball to short.

In one easy movement, Danny scooped it up and pegged the ball home. A perfect throw! Larry tagged Drew out and sped the ball back to third, but he was too late. With two away, the bases were still loaded.

No mistakes, said Danny to himself. No mistakes. He hunkered down, eyes glued to home plate.

The tension of the moment proved to be too much for Roy Feenie, the next batter. He struck out.

The game was over: Bullets 5–Jaguars 2.

Danny was jubilant as he jogged off the field. They were still in the running! The series was tied 2–2 — and Danny knew his playing today had helped bring about the much needed victory.

Tammy had been left on deck when the game ended. She'd been talking to one of her teammates and was still on the diamond near home as Danny passed by. Before he could stop to think of what he was doing, he called out "Nice homer" and kept moving.

Tammy whirled around and shouted, "What's *that* supposed to mean? Rubbing it in?"

Danny stopped in his tracks. "I just meant you really clobbered that ball."

"Oh, sure, you really *meant* that," she said angrily. "Don't think I haven't noticed you checking me out. You've been mimicking my every move. What are you trying to do, copy the way I play so you can beat me for the All-Star spot? Fat chance! And I saw you taking pictures, too."

Danny just stood there, speechless, as she went on.

"Well, you can forget about looking for my weak spot, 'cause I don't have one. I'm just as good as you are!" she snapped.

And then it happened. Danny stared her straight in the eyes and said calmly, "You should be. After all, we're twins."

11

Tammy stared back at him. She didn't even blink at first. But all the color drained from her face. Then she broke into tears and ran off the field.

Danny was stunned by her reaction. But he was too upset with himself to go after her. How could he have just blurted something like that out?

"What's going on, Danny? You act like you just got through talking to a vampire," said Joel, coming over to him. "Your new girlfriend give you a hard time, there?"

"She's not my girlfriend, Joel," said Danny tiredly. "Let's get changed and I'll explain it to you."

On the way home, Danny filled Joel in on what had happened, how he'd suspected something, and how his mother finally told him the story.

"Your *twin sister*? Wow! That really is wild," said Joel. "Wait till the guys hear about this!"

"Hold on for a minute," said Danny. "Maybe we better not let anyone know until after the series. Look at what happened when I told her! They might not know how to handle it either."

"You sure?" asked Joel.

"I'm sure," said Danny. "What I can't figure out is how to let her know that I'm not mad at her or anything."

"You'll figure that out," said Joel.

When he got home, he told his parents what had happened. They were dismayed at first, but then they decided that while the *way* Danny had told Tammy wasn't the best, it was good that the truth was out once and for all.

Danny thought about nothing else for the rest of the day. Finally, he decided he would write Tammy a letter and tell her the way he told Joel, the whole story and how he found out. That ought to make her understand that he wasn't spying on her or anything like that.

"*Dear Tammy,*" he began.

For the next half hour he scribbled away, trying to

find the right words to let her know how he felt and how he didn't know how to feel, all at the same time.

Finally, he had finished the letter.

Dear Tammy,

I'm sorry about the way I told you about us being twins. I was going to wait until after the series was over because it looks like baseball is as important to you as it is to me — and I figured finding out the truth might break your concentration. As much as I want to win this series and make the All-Star team, I would never try to do something bad to you. I mean, you're one of the best players out there. I thought I was a shoo-in for the All-Star spot until I saw you play. I guess that's why I've been watching you so closely. At first that was why, anyway. But the more I saw the way you played baseball — throwing righty but batting lefty, your stance at the plate, the way you run and field the ball — the more I saw that we share more than just good playing ability. Then other things started adding up. Weird coincidences like both of us being adopted (Okay, I admit I looked up your game stats in some old newspapers, so maybe I was spying a little bit!). And I couldn't believe it when I heard your team sing "Happy Birthday" to you on my birthday! Anyway, I finally asked my mom about it, and she told me the truth.

Believe it or not, I really like the idea that we're sister and brother, even though you are threatening to push me out of the All-Star spot. I hope you can forgive me and that we can get to know each other someday.

Good luck in Saturday's game. May the best person and team win.

Sincerely,
Danny Walker

"There, that's the best I can do," he said to the empty room. "Now I need an envelope so I can mail it to her first thing tomorrow. Where'd I put that package of envelopes Jennifer gave me?"

"Danny! Dinner's ready," his father called from downstairs.

I'll get the envelope later, he thought as he left his room.

The smell of garlic and butter greeted him as he entered the kitchen.

"Oh, boy, garlic bread!" he exclaimed. "I could eat a whole loaf."

"Not a good idea," said Jennifer, nibbling on a small piece. "Fattening."

"Danny doesn't have to worry," said Mr. Walker. "And neither do you. At your age, you both burn it off real fast."

Mrs. Walker passed around a platter of sliced roast chicken, baked potatoes, and a bowl of green beans with slivers of almond.

Danny heaped his plate with everything that came his way.

"This is definitely one of my favorite meals, Mom. How come?" he asked, looking up at her. He noticed that she had red-rimmed eyes, but there were no tears.

"You know that we always celebrate birthdays three days before and three days after," she said. "We're just stretching things a little."

Conversation stopped while the food was being passed. It didn't quite catch on afterward as it usually did. Then Mr. Walker cleared his throat and said, "I think you ought to know that we've just spoken to the Aikens, Danny."

"You *did*?" he asked.

"We called them and told them about what had happened," Mr. Walker said. "Your mother tried to explain everything that she could."

"Uh-huh," Danny said, nodding. "What about Tammy? That article about her in the *Jamestown Journal* sports section said she was adopted, so she must've known that. Did . . . did *she* know she had a twin brother?"

"Actually, she did," said Mrs. Walker. "Her parents told her about it when they were living out west. At the time it seemed so unlikely that you two children would ever meet up, they felt they could say something. I wish — I only wish we had, too."

"It's okay, Mom," said Danny. "I wish I'd known, too, but then again, maybe it was better that I saw Tammy first. Otherwise, I might not have believed it — or I might have wondered if every red-haired girl I met was my twin!"

"Well, now she knows who her twin brother is," said Jennifer, dropping a bare chicken wing bone on her plate. "Talk about a 'duel on the diamond!' I mean, it's really freaky that you're both shortstops, too. If I had a twin — I don't, right?" she asked. "I mean, if I had a twin brother, I'd want him to be a movie star or a rock singer."

"Sorry, but you don't, so he's not. You have a regular brother, and he's a wonderful baseball player, among other things," said Mrs. Walker, smiling. "So just help Danny clear the plates, and the two of you can take the pie out of the fridge."

"Pie? What kind?" asked Danny.

"Blueberry," said Mrs. Walker. "And yes, there's vanilla ice cream in the freezer, too."

Danny knew for sure then that this was a really special meal.

As he stacked the plates and tossed the forks and knives on top, he stopped in his tracks.

"Mom," he said. "Did the Walkers say anything about how Tammy feels now? You know, now that she knows who I am?"

"They didn't," said Mr. Walker. "Apparently, she hasn't spoken to them about it."

Mrs. Walker added, "They think it best to just leave her alone to sort out her feelings without any hint of pressure from them."

Danny nodded. "Sounds like we have more in common than just baseball," he said.

But that didn't really answer his question. He kept seeing the look on Tammy's face when she was accusing him of spying on her. And then the way she paled when he'd blurted out the truth.

He knew what he had to do.

"Mom? Can I have an envelope — and a postage stamp?" he asked.

Later on that evening, he strolled into Jennifer's room. She was sitting in her rocking chair surrounded by about two million stuffed animals, wearing headphones.

He tapped her on top of the head lightly. "Hello? Anybody home?" he asked.

She took off the headphones. He could hear an electric guitar and some real loud clanging still coming out of them until she turned off her stereo.

"Some day, huh?" she said. "You okay?"

"Yeah, though it still feels a little weird," he said.

"I can't imagine what Tammy's thinking," said Jennifer.

"Yeah, me either," said Danny. "Boy, she sure lit into me before I spilled the beans!"

116

"Why?" Jennifer asked. "What was her beef?"

"Oh, a bunch of stuff," said Danny. "I mean she thought that I thought — well, I straightened that out."

"You did?" asked Jennifer. "How?"

"I wrote to her," he said.

"You *what*? Are you nuts?"

"I figured she ought to hear my side of the story, and why I've been so interested in her and everything. I sure would if it were me."

Jennifer shook her head. "This may be none of my business, but I'll tell you one thing."

"What?"

"I think she needs a little breathing room to figure this out by herself. A letter from you could be the last thing Tammy wants right now. Sorry, buddy, but you may have really screwed up."

The sky was filled with puffy white clouds the morning of the fifth and final game of the championship series between the Jaguars and the Bullets. But they scattered away before long, and the sun shone brightly down on the well-mown grass of the diamond.

Danny arrived at the field for warm-up a little early. He thought he might get a chance to "accidentally" bump into Tammy and see how she felt. But the Jaguars stayed well over to one side and the Bullets kept to the other. There weren't even any stray balls to chase into enemy territory as an excuse.

Danny noticed that Joel was working hard to act natural — even though he was in on the big secret. But when he threw his arm around Danny's shoulders and yelled, "Hey, buddy-boy, how's it going?" for the fourth time that afternoon, Danny was sure his teammates would sense something was going on. Fortunately, they were all used to odd behavior from Joel.

"Give me a break," said Joanne, stomping off toward the dugout.

Danny shook his head and, serious as he was, laughed at Joel. That helped break some of the tension.

The Jaguars took to the field as the Bullets came up to bat. Danny got into position on the bench to move up when his turn came. But Coach Lattizori called him over and said, "Danny, take it easy for a while. You're going to play, but I want to have a few of my big guns ready for later on in the game."

Danny's heart sank. He understood the coach's strategy. It was something he did all the time. But what if this game was crucial to Danny's chances of making the county All-Stars? He needed to be out there or else — or else someone else would be chosen. And that someone would probably be his own twin sister, Tammy Aiken.

Do the best you can. Do the best you can.

He'd heard those words of advice all his life. This was going to really put him to the test. Now he had to wait for his turn to play and do his best — no matter what else was happening on the field.

Vern, who was back on second base, led off for the Bullets. Andy Hooten was on the mound for the Jaguars.

Andy was a little nervous and sent Vern to first on a walk. But he held off Elaine, who was up next. With an 0 and 2 count, she got too far under the next pitch and popped it out to third.

Next Danny watched Mike, playing third and batting third, go down swinging for the second out. Then Ken Hunter came up and took the second walk to first base. With two runners on bases and two outs, Frankie Snow came up to the plate.

Danny wanted the Bullets to win. He wanted Frankie to get a hit and send Vern or Ken — or both — home. But he also wished he was up at bat now, like he usually was.

He pushed those thoughts out of his mind.

Frankie did his best, but he failed to connect. After a swing and a miss, a called strike, and two really high pitches, he went for a breaker and missed it for strike three and out three.

The Jaguars did better in the first inning of play. Joey Sands set the pace with a double to right field. Wally popped up for the first out, but Marsha followed with a beauty of a line drive down the middle that went deep into center field. It was enough to take Joey home though Marsha stayed on first. The Jaguars had drawn first blood again and were on the scoreboard 1–0.

Marc Bailey, pitching for the Bullets, struck out Roy Feenie. Tammy came up to bat.

It was the first chance Danny had to take a close look at her this game. Had she gotten his letter, and if so, what was her reaction?

Then Tammy made contact with the ball, and Danny snapped back to attention. Tammy arrived safely on first, Marsha moved up to second — and Danny reminded himself that during a game, Tammy was just another player. And a threatening one at that.

With two runners on base and two outs, Al Norris hit a line drive straight into Vern's waiting glove to end the inning.

Joanne led off for the Bullets in the second.

"Come on, Joanne. We want a hit!"

"Let's go, Bullets!"

The shouts from the Bullets' fans rang out as she stepped into the batter's box.

She didn't disappoint them. The ball flew into short left field for a stand-up single.

Danny called out to Joel, who was leaving the on-deck circle, "Show 'em what you've got, Joel!"

It could have been that Andy Hooten didn't want to see what Joel had. He walked the Bullets' center fielder.

That brought up Larry Chuan, who was also capable of hitting the big one. The outfield stayed deep as he got set at the plate.

Larry let the first pitch go by for a called strike, then went for the next. He hit a line drive, which Marsha caught for the out. A fast peg to first caught Joel off base for another.

Joanne had advanced to third, where she held up. Her chances of scoring were dimmed by Marc's arrival in the batter's box. It didn't take many pitches before he struck out to end the inning for the Bullets.

With a one-run lead, the Jaguars didn't do much better that inning. Drew and Millie got on base with ground ball singles, but Andy struck out. And then Joey Sands let his team down by hitting into a double play.

Two double plays in one inning made the fans uneasy. As the Jaguars took to the field and the Bullets came in, there were boos and catcalls mixed with the cheers.

Things got even worse in the top of the third. As Danny squirmed around on the bench, he watched the Bullets put two runners on with one out — and again hit into a double play, *their* second one that game. He wished he could be out there doing something to help the team. But he knew he'd have to wait until the coach was ready to make the move. So far Frankie's fielding had been okay.

But the bottom of the third proved to be a rough one for the Bullets. Marc started off by walking Wally. Marsha then popped out to Frankie, who tried to pick off Wally on second, but missed. Then, with the runner on second, Roy Feenie suddenly found the perfect pitch.

Crack!

It sailed over the left field fence for a home run. That made the score Jaguars 3–Bullets 0.

There was no more action on the bases. Her second time at bat, Tammy struck out. She was followed by Al Norris, who hit a hard one deep into left field. Joel picked it off right next to the fence for the final out.

Frankie was due to lead off, but Coach Lattizori called over to Danny.

"Grab your helmet and get out there," said the coach. "Let's get a little action going. All we want is a hit to start things off, Danny. Just do your stuff."

Danny's "stuff" was his reliability. He didn't disappoint. He let three inside pitches go by for a 3 and 0 count. Andy had to give him something now.

It was a fastball down the middle. Danny swung and connected with a sizzling line drive that went between short and third. It was good enough to put him on second base.

He breathed a sigh of relief and glanced over to short. Tammy didn't even look in his direction. Maybe she doesn't realize it's me here on second, he thought. Or maybe, he added dismally, she knows but doesn't care. His heart turned cold at the thought.

Joanne stepped into the batter's box next. The Jaguars' outfield backed up a little, and she took advantage of it by belting a line drive that sent center and right scrambling in. Danny took off the minute he heard bat connect with ball. He beat the throw home for the Bullets' first run of the game. He waved his cap triumphantly at Joanne, who had made it to first without any trouble.

The rally slowed a little when Joel Jackson struck out. But Larry Chuan redeemed himself by hitting a ground ball that almost reached the right field fence before Millie Albright stopped it. Joanne was on her way home for the Bullets' second run. The peg at second was too late, so Larry stretched his hit to a triple.

Then Marc hit an easy grounder to first and was tagged out. Larry held tight at third. Vern Labar came up to bat, looking to make his mark on the game. He let two outside balls go by, then reached for one that was a little closer in. He connected with a line drive that sailed over short and landed him safe on first. Larry crossed the plate for the Bullets' third run of the inning.

That run turned out to be their last. Elaine struck out, and the top of the fourth was over with the score now tied, 3–3.

Danny felt sharp and alert as he headed out to the field for the bottom of the inning. It was a brand-new ball game to him, and he was determined to make the most of it.

He got his wish right off when Drew Ferris, leading off for the Jaguars, hit one straight into his mitt for the first out. Then Millie came up to the plate. Marc had her number, too, giving her nothing great to swing at. She finally took an inside ball for a grounder straight down the first base line. Joanne pulled it in and made the tag for out number two.

Having hit the ball in the second inning, Andy Hooten was all set to do it again. But he went down swinging, and the fourth inning ended with the score still tied.

"Okay, you Bullets, take it away!" shouted Jennifer from the stands. Danny could always make out her voice.

Mike Worsley was hoping to start a rally, but he

ended up waiting out four bad pitches for a walk. Ken popped one to the pitcher for out number one.

Then Danny came up to bat. The noise from the stands made it clear that he was a great favorite with the Bullets' fans.

He cleared his mind of everything. The round white horsehide with the red stitching shot toward him from the pitcher's mound.

The first pitch was high. Ball one. The second was low. Ball two. The third was right down the middle.

He swung hard and hit the ball deep into center field. It sailed way over the head of Al Norris, who hadn't played him deep enough. But Al recovered the ball quickly and pegged it all the way home. That kept Mike on third and Danny on second with only one out.

The Bullets would take the lead if Joanne could send Mike home. But she lobbed a high foul ball that the Jaguars' catcher, Drew Ferris, put away on the third base line. Mike hugged close to the third base bag.

Joel Jackson came up to bat and tried to do the job but failed. He popped one out to short, and Tammy put it away for the final out.

She's playing a real steady game, Danny thought as he ran out to the field. He wasn't positive, but he thought he caught her glance in his direction as she came in. She looked away before he had a chance to react.

The top of the Jaguars' batting order led off in the bottom of the fifth inning. Still smarting from hitting into a double play, Joey Sands looked ready to redeem himself. But he went for a low pitch that bobbled down the first base line for the first out.

Wally didn't do much better, hitting a grounder that Mike captured for the second out.

Then Marsha started a rally with a double that Danny almost tagged out but missed by a hair. With a runner on second base, Marc walked the next batter, Roy Feenie, which brought up Tammy.

Danny suddenly found himself praying that she wouldn't hit the ball his way. I'd hate to ruin it for my own twin sister, he thought, whether she knows it or not. But I will if I have to.

He breathed a sigh of relief when Tammy belted the ball into deep right field. She made it to first as Marsha slid into home.

Marc managed to put Al Norris away with three

straight called strikes. Still, the inning had ended with the score now Jaguars 4–Bullets 3.

It was the last inning and the last chance for the Bullets to run up a big enough score to win the game.

Can we do it? Danny wondered as he watched Larry go to the plate. Can Larry get on base and come home for the tying run?

He got part of an answer when Larry took his base on a walk.

Marc provided a little more excitement. The Bullets' pitcher surprised his teammates by hitting a clean single into left field. Larry stretched his run to third. He was now in scoring position.

But Andy Hooten wasn't about to give up right then and there. He struck out Vern and Elaine one after the other with a series of dazzling pitches.

And that's when he started his downslide. He walked Mike to load the bases — and then walked the next batter, Ken Hunter, to tie the game.

The fans went wild cheering for both sides as the Jaguars' coach walked out to the mound for a talk with Andy. After a moment of discussion, the coach walked back and Andy stayed in to face Danny.

Danny had gotten hits his two previous times at

bat. Now he faced a field with the bases loaded, two outs, and the game tied in the sixth and final inning.

Just do your best, he said to himself. Forget everything else and just do your best.

Okay, here goes, he thought. He stepped into the batter's box, choked up on the bat, and crouched into a comfortable hitting position. Oh, for a good one, he begged silently.

He got his wish on the first pitch. It was a little bit outside and just above the middle. He swung hard and connected.

The ball went bounding down the field toward second and short. Danny dropped the bat and started to run. Out of the corner of his eye, he saw Tammy move to stop the ball.

But as he charged toward first, Danny heard the crowd gasp in astonishment. His own eyes widened in disbelief when he saw the first baseman make a desperate leap to try to catch a wild throw. The next thing he knew, he was safe. A run had scored, and only a great stop and throw by Roy Feenie kept a second runner from crossing the plate.

"What happened?" Danny asked the first base coach as the umpire tried to quiet the crowd down.

"The shortstop flubbed the pickup and then threw a wild one to first!" was the reply.

"You don't know how lucky you are to be standing here," growled the first baseman. "Tammy's *never* done that before."

The officials ruled it an error, but the run scored, and the Bullets were now ahead, 5–4.

As Danny stood on base, he had to wonder: Was it an error? Was she just nervous? Or was it something she did on purpose to make him look good?

He planned on getting a good look at Tammy's face when he got closer to see if he could tell. But Joanne popped one out to right field to end the inning, and he didn't get a chance.

Before taking the field for the bottom of the sixth, the Bullets huddled near their bench. They joined hands in the center of a circle and let out a loud war cry. Then they ran off to their positions.

This is it, Danny realized, heart thumping. If we hold them now, we win the championship. If I don't mess up, I have a great shot at county All-Star now that Tammy's blown it with that error.

He forced himself to take it one batter at a time. That started off with Drew, who hit one deep into center field. Joel was under it and put it away for the first out.

Then Millie came up and got her first hit of the game, a ground ball to third that she outran for a single.

With time running out and a run behind, a pinch hitter went in for Andy Hooten. Again it was Barney Gold who stepped into the batter's box. Danny could practically feel Barney's hunger as the burly outfielder stared down the line at Marc on the mound.

Marc's first pitch was a fastball that went for a called strike. The next one was a little slower, and Barney saw it coming. He belted it into deep left field. Ken stopped it on a bounce and pegged it to third. The runners held on first and second.

Then Joey Sands came up to bat. Joey hadn't looked all that sharp since hitting into a double play in the third inning. He never was much of a power hitter, so the Bullets' infield came in a little for the play.

The first pitch was a little low, but he swung at it — and missed. The next two were high and outside for a 2–1 count.

And then a breaking pitch came his way and Joey gave it everything he had.

Crack!

The ball sailed high into the air, out toward left field. It kept on going, going, and was gone — over the fence for a three-run home run!

The Jaguars streamed out of the dugout, cheering and whooping as each of the runners cross the plate. Danny watched as the scoreboard changed one last time. The final score read Jaguars 7, Bullets 5. The Jaguars had taken the series, 3–2.

Danny knew that there was a good chance that his baseball season would get an extension. Tammy's error all but sealed his spot on the All-Star team. But the end of the series meant that he and Tammy would no longer be forced together. Would that be the end of it?

The crowd spilled onto the field and crowded around the players on both teams. But before they could go off to their respective dugout areas, the Jaguars and the Bullets met on the mount to exchange handshakes.

When they came to each other, Danny and Tammy lowered their eyes. They put out their hands and withdrew them after a brief touch. Danny started to move on. But then he realized that Tammy hadn't budged. She continued to stare at the ground with her hands hanging at her sides. He stepped back. She raised her head and met his eyes. There was a moment of stony silence. Then they both broke out in identical wide smiles. In the next second, they had wrapped their arms around each other in a warm and loving hug.

Of course, they tripped up half the team on each side as they stood there. Jaguars and Bullets stumbled all over them. Joel Jackson bumped into them and cried out, "Looks like double trouble at short to me!"

The twin shortstops burst into laughter and walked off the field arm in arm.

Matt Christopher

Kobe Bryant	*Randy Johnson*
Terrell Davis	*Michael Jordan*
John Elway	*Lisa Leslie*
Julie Foudy	*Tara Lipinski*
Jeff Gordon	*Mark McGwire*
Wayne Gretzky	*Greg Maddux*
Ken Griffey Jr.	*Hakeem Olajuwon*
Mia Hamm	*Briana Scurry*
Tony Hawk	*Sammy Sosa*
Grant Hill	*Tiger Woods*
Derek Jeter	*Steve Young*

The #1 Sports Series for Kids

Read them all!

All available in paperback from Little, Brown and Company